Sinfullicious
Platinum Edition

Angelic Artiaga

The New Face of Pure Erotica

A Series Written by: Angelic Artiaga

Published by: Martin & Bloomberg, Inc.

Cover Design/Graphics: Gold Starr Entertainment, Inc.

Editors: Maariyah Artiaga

Facebook.com/WriterAngelicArtiaga

Twitter: @AngelicArtiaga

ISBN-13: **978-0692621523**

FOR THE FEATHER IN MY HAT...

"I don't mind working, holding my ground intellectually, artistically; but as a woman, oh, God, as a woman I want to be dominated. I don't mind being told to stand on my own feet, not to cling, be all that I am capable of doing, but I am going to be pursued, fucked, possessed by the will of a male at his time, his bidding." ...Anias Nin

CONTENTS

DISCLAIMER

SHADOWY FIGURE

He was still standing in our master bathroom buttoning his shirt. Tall, strong, beautiful brown skin. He was so sexy, all man! Every woman's fantasy.

I stood from our bed, "It's 11:30 babe." I walked over to him, buttoned his last button.

He looked down at me, kissed me on my forehead. "Yeah, I know."

"Well since you know," I smiled, "don't you think you should hurry it up!"

He walked into our bedroom, grabbed his keys from the nightstand. "I'm going... I'm going."

I went and sat on the side of our bed. "Your lunch is waiting on the counter."

He came back to me, leaned over for one last kiss. "Gimmie kiss. Gotta go. Running late."

"Please don't get another speeding ticket."

"I won't. Love you."

I watched him disappear through our bedroom door, whispered to the back of his head, "I love you too..."

He sprinted down the stairs and through the kitchen. A second later I heard him turn the lock on the front door.

He was gone and I was all alone; again.

My husband had to be at work by midnight and he frequently pressed his luck by running late.

He was a serious workaholic. Worked seven days a week, sometimes twelve hours a day.

After he left, I stood from our bed and went down stairs.

1

Obsessed with safety I did my usual routine, checked and double-checked all of the windows and door locks.

We lived in a big house in the secluded suburbs. Our neighborhood was lined with track homes, manicured lawns, and community cluster mail box units at the end of each street. Unlike in the inner city, the crime rate in our neighborhood was zero. None of our windows wore bars, and the only barriers surrounding our houses were the redwood fences separating our back yards. Still, I always felt the need to check all locks.

Satisfied that all was secure, I went to the pantry and grabbed a bag of microwave popcorn. I pushed 2 on the ovens express timer and stood there listening to the kernels exploding against the ballooning bag. At the first beep I grabbed the hot bag from the oven, hit the kitchen light, and hurried upstairs to my bed.

Kettle corn in hand, I crawled into our king sized bed and slid my thin reading glasses over my Asian eyes.

I really hated being home alone, and especially at night; so I'd made it my ritual to have that little snack to keep me company. My husband told me that I needed to stop being a silly chicken, that I was too old to be afraid of the dark.

I pinched the corners of the bag and then pulled them apart. Let the sweet steam rise to my nose and fog my narrow lenses.

Ahh... kettle corn to the rescue.

Snack in hand, hair twisted up, reading glasses on my face, I curled up with one of my favorite books – a sinful edition of romance and lust - and let pages of erotica take me away.

Munching on my company, I read chapter after chapter. The pleasures and spirituality of Kama Sutra entertained me for about an hour before setting my book and popcorn on my nightstand. I turned the knob on my headboard dimming the overhead light, and then buried my tired head into my pile of pillows.

Lying there in silence, I did what I had been doing since I was a little girl; I said my prayers, peaceful words in my native tongue Japanese, and then I fell into a nice sleep.

A few dreams later, I was awaken by a loud bang! That sound

was startling, sent my eyes flying wide open.

Oh my God! What was that?

I threw my eyes toward the red numbers hovering over my nightstand; it was only 4 am.

Something had fallen downstairs.

It sounded like something big and heavy, maybe one of our wooden barstools tumbling over and slamming onto the kitchen tiled floor.

I laid there for a few seconds, paralyzed with fear, eyes glued to my opened bedroom doorway, staring into the empty and now quiet darkness.

I reached for my cell phone and powered it on; 911 at the ready.

I wanted to get up, close and lock my bedroom door. But if I'd done that I wouldn't have been able to hear what may be going on downstairs, to hear what may be coming up the stairs toward me.

I didn't move, held my breath, and listened carefully.

I was as quiet, as quiet as whoever or whatever had come into my house.

Ears leading my other four senses, showing me things that my eyes couldn't see, determining what I should do next.

Within a few moments I started hearing other things that I've never paid any attention to; like the wind lightly blowing outside of my bedroom window and the traffic traveling along the freeway from about a mile away, and then there was this buzzing or a ringing in my ears; the sound of the house's electricity.

My bionic hearing started seeing things that were no threat to me; the pounding of my heart beating inside my chest, and the blood rushing and drumming in my ears.

After a few minutes of listening to nothing moving in the house, I figured that whatever my ears saw while I was asleep must have been something I heard in my dreams. Or, it was just another episode of me being me, of me being my usual scared self.

I really wish I didn't have to be alone in this big damn empty house... At night... Every night.

I told myself it was just my imagination and that I should just go back to sleep.

And so I tried.

I tried hard, but couldn't get there.

I lifted my head, looked over at the clock again, only five minutes had passed. It was going to be at least eight more hours before my husband got off work, and at least eight and a half before he made it home.

I could've called him, but then he would've just preached to me about being so spooked over nothing. He would have reminded me of how I needed to stop and that I was once again being silly. But besides all that, I really didn't want to bother him at work. So I decided to do the next best thing.

I rolled over to my other side, ran my hand across his pillow and pulled it close to me. I inhaled his scent, whispered his name, and that made me feel like my husband was close to me. As if he was right there, protecting me.

Still wide awake and unable to shake that uneasy feeling, I sat up and reached for the TV remote.

I channel surfed, nothing good on at that hour. Every channel seemed to be showing some sort of X-Rated B movie or lying infomercial, and I hated infomercials. Everything on display was new and improved, the next best thing, came with a money back guarantee, and if I called right then, I could get a second one for free. All I needed to do was to pay shipping and handling.

Ugh!

I pushed power, clicked the TV off, and tossed the remote aside.

Still thinking about the sound that I had hoped was just my imagination, I couldn't help but to go back to listening. I listened to the air and the only new thing that I heard was a sizzling sound, the white noise that came to life as power dissolved from the television screen. It's funny how that static electricity is not really a sound but is actually a feeling, something tickling your eardrums, tricking them into believing that they are hearing things, doing precisely what I hoped my mind was doing to me right then.

I spoke to myself. Just say another prayer, and go back to sleep.

I closed my eyes, loosened my grip on my cell phone and let it relax on the bed beside me. Psalms 23... The Lord is my Sheppard...

But then, just as I relaxed, I heard a new sound.

A rustling noise.

One that felt close to me. Too close to me.

This time the sound was real and I knew it. I had not fallen back asleep so I knew that I wasn't dreaming that time. I was hearing a real sound and it was not coming from outside of my window nor from anywhere downstairs.

This time is was right next to me.

It was a sound made by something, or someone. A sound made inside of my bedroom.

My eyes flew open and swept my bedroom. I looked around the perimeter, examining carefully.

And that's when it happened.

My eyes landed on what looked like a mountain. A large shadowy figure standing at the foot of my bed!

Head spinning, mind moving faster than the speed of thought, I sat straight up, almost emptied my bladder in my bed.

A sudden surge of panic powered by adrenaline rushed straight through me, made me break into a cold sweat, my muscles contract, and caused me to violently tremble.

My greatest fears had broken through all of my safety precautions. My worst nightmare was standing right in front of me, a monster that went bump in the night was now standing at the foot of my bed!

I wanted to scream, to sound the alarms, but fear constricted my vocal cords.

Eyes glued to the shadowy figure, I eased a trembling hand

across my bed, searched between the sheets, feeling for my cell phone.

That's when I nudged it.

My fingertips in a frenzy pushed my cell phone over the edge. I saw my life flash before my eyes. My help had fallen hard, like a brick landing with a loud thud.

I swallowed hard. Oh God no.

My phone's thud was as loud as the bomb that hit Hiroshima. In that moment my immediate plan went up in smoke, and I imagined what was to come; his horrible invasion of my Japan.

I had no weapons and now no way to call for help. I was so scared. I didn't know what to do. My eyes flew to my bedroom door and then snapped back to him. The shadowy figure was not moving, was just standing there, looking at me. His frame reaching about six and a half feet high, about three feet wide, he was like Michael Meyers in those Halloween movies.

I blinked. Examined him.

The figure was so still I started to wonder what it was. Was it human, or was it a big black ghost?

Finally, and after what seemed like an eternity, it moved.

It shifted to the left, its body struck by a finger of moonlight. And then, to my dismay, I realized that it was not a ghost. This was a solid figure, a real man.

A big, tall, shirtless man wearing only a black mask and gloves, and what looked like dark colored sweat pants.

I let out a loud scream and that made him flinch.

When I saw that he was rattled, I tried to make a run for it. Without a second thought I jumped from my bed. But before my feet could make a solid landing, his gloved fingers were tangled in my hair.

He tossed me back onto my bed, threw my screaming body like it was a small ragdoll, and then he growled at me, told me to shut up!

But I couldn't shut up. I had finally found my voice and I couldn't stop screaming.

I inhaled deeply and screamed again. Let out screams of bloody murder, screams riding on tidal waves of terror. I conjured screams loud enough to shatter all silence, enough to wake all things sleeping in our quiet suburban neighborhood.

His voice raised as high as mine, told me to shut my fucking mouth and do exactly what he says! His bass boomed from the foot of my bed as he barked at me through an oval shaped hole in his mask.

I scurried away from him, backpedaled toward the top of my bed and pulled my knees in close into my chest. My eyes wanted to travel back toward my darkened escape route but I willed them to stay locked on my adversary.

My eyes scaling the mountain of a man standing so close to me. I thought I was going to have a heart attack.

I looked toward the floor in the direction of my fallen cell phone, I had 911 on speed dial.

I put my eyes back on him and then started inching toward the side of the bed. But right away he realized what I was trying to do.

He balled up both fists and said, "Don't even think about it." His tone was so cruel and threatening, it tied my body into a knot.

I shook my head fast. "Please don't hurt me... Please don't!" Eyes burning with salty tears, I begged him.

The shadowy figure was like a towering statue, unmoving. His eyes peering at me through two small holes carved into his knitted mask. He stood there stiff and still, peeping-tomming at me.

As if he didn't hear me the first time, I pled louder. "Please! What do you want from me?"

He said something back, but he said it in a voice too low for me to hear. I don't know what he said, but his mumbling scared the shit out of me.

I pulled my crumpled sheets and comforter over my knees, and started crying.

In a standoff, we sized each other up. There was no way I

could win this battle against him. I was a petite young bride, had only been married for under a year. The scent living between my legs was still sweet and smelled almost virgin.

He was large. His mask was concealing his age. But by the looks of his sturdy frame, the strength in his hands, how he tossed me effortlessly onto my bed, he had to have been pretty young.

Suddenly, like a gust of wind, he raced toward the right of my bed. And in an attempt to get away I scrambled as fast as I could to the left.

But he moved across the room in seconds, with a velocity that was unreal. He grabbed my leg and pulled me back across the bed toward him. A moment later his heavy silhouette on top of me. Both my wrist bound by one of his gloved hands as he lifted my thin nightgown with the other.

My eyes at my ceiling, my nostrils burned with his masculine scent as he prepared to enslave me. His gloved finger went to the crotch of my panties, pulled them aside, and then tore them off me.

Fear ripped through me just like the laced panties he had stolen from my body.

Sweating and shaking, I tried stiffening my thighs. I used all of my might to lift him off of me, all my strength to close my legs, but his strong body wedged between my thighs made that mission impossible. I had to do something, needed to try something else.

I prayed. Asked God for help.

That's when my alpha female entered the room and started appealing to his alpha male, did what the strongest woman would have done. Let female tears speak through soft and delicate pleading.

I used feminine powers against masculine strength. I asked him why he was doing this to me. I asked him why me? Why me?

With a stoic voice he told me to be quiet, that he had heard it all before.

Oh my God...oh my God.

This was how it always happened, crimes unrecognized in good neighborhoods like mine. I lived in the suburbs, the land where serial killers were born, bred, and ran free.

His next move was poignant, not to be misconstrued.

He reached down and unzipped his pants.

I squirmed and kicked to no avail.

As his zippers teeth unlocked, I thought about my husband, about my family and friends, about living or dying after this man was finished doing whatever he was going to do to me.

His heavy penis fell out of his zipper and grazed my inner thigh.

I twisted and wiggled, strained to break free. But he was much too strong, incredibly heavy.

I screamed, "Please! Please don't do this to me!" My voice rippled through sobs and tears. Still, none of that moved him. He stayed his course.

He took hold of himself, swiped his hot flesh against my inner thigh.

He said, "I promise you're going to love this." and before I could form the words calling him a liar, the head of his erection was breaking my skin.

I tried arching my back and pressing my hips into the bed, tightening my opening, trying not to let him in, but his desires were like a locomotive that I didn't have the strength to stop.

He moved past my ring of privacy, at a rhythm that felt good to him, a rhythm that was somewhat alien to me, one that made me feel so violated.

His glove went up to my neck, started choking me. He pressed his nose against my cheek, whispered that he wanted to make love to me. Told me that he should make love to me but that he knew that wasn't what I really wanted.

He stuck his tongue through the hole in the mask and licked up the side of my face.

I wrestled with him, struggled with him, and tried to scream again, but he squeezed my throat harder, wouldn't let me inhale enough oxygen.

Mouth open, gasping for air, my tongue crawled out of my mouth.

He was fucking me, kissing me, licking my tongue. I was still shaking, crying, struggling to break free.

He gave me deep kisses and deep penetration and I could do nothing about it.

He finally slid his tongue out past my lips, and then I gasped and repeated, "Please stop…" I shook my head, gasped again, "Please… please." I couldn't think of any words other than please, and so I just kept repeating that same word.

He said, "I've been watching you… watching me."

Heaving, his frame heavy on top of mine, I struggled to catch my breath.

His thrust became slower, each one more deliberate. He said, "This is what you get for lusting after me," and then he shoved his tongue into my mouth again, the rough edges of his mask abrasive against my lips.

I tried focusing, calculating every word he was saying. I wanted to understand what was going on inside of his sick mind. I needed to formulate a plan, to come up with a strategy of what I should do in order to get away from him. Right then the reality TV show, 'I survived', came into my head. I did my best to remember what I had learned, but he was assaulting me and so nothing computed into anything that made sense. He was going so deep I thought my insides were going to explode. I was trying to think, but he was fucking the common sense out of me.

I had to keep it together. Otherwise I could have possibly not made it out alive. So I disappeared, surrendered to his fast and hard thrusts, to his moans and vulgar words.

I set my mind free, did what lots of survivors have done, and that allowed me to come up with the start of what felt like a real plan.

Rule number one: Don't do anything else to upset him.

He groaned in my ear, "You want me don't you?"

Rule number two: Humanize yourself to him

My mind told me to think carefully before I speak, to use extreme caution with every word.

His tone was scathing, his scent reminiscing, breath steamy, like warm bathwater licking at the side of my neck.

He whispered between thrusts, "You want it like this... right? This is what you've been looking for... right?"

His body punishing mine, I answered his menacing questions, said, "I don't know."

I didn't want to deny his claim but I didn't want to encourage him either. I could only think to be as polite as I possibly could. If I wanted to live, I dared not risk pissing him off again.

He let out a sharp laugh, made another change in his body's rhythm.

He said, "Don't lie to me. You know damn well what you want!" and with that he added speed and power to his hip's pace.

His thrashing was frightening. My legs pried wide, his body weight was crushing. I almost lost it. With my small frame buried beneath his, my mind argued with me, told me to be smart and to hold my position.

I tried striking him with a new kind of pity. "No... no... please stop... you're killing me..." my voice exhausted, trailed off into a world of whimpering whispers.

My begging him to stop had turned something on inside of him, and confirmed that with what he did next. He pulled away from me, readjusted himself, handed me a sly grin.

His gloved hands lifted me by my thighs and flipped me over.

On my face, he grabbed me by my waist and lifted me onto my knees. His leathered fingers crawled my waist, and then tilted my ass upward toward the ceiling.

He paused. Inhaled the view. I cringed at the thought of what he might do next.

My face was buried in a pile of pillows while his erection danced in front of my opening.

All that was mine was about to become his.

That's when I made what I believed to be a brave decision. I tried to hit him hard with a backwards kick. But then he caught my foot in midair, flipped me back over. That maneuver of mine completely pissed him off, made him threaten me with something else. He told me to stop fighting him, or else.

He was so strong but by that point, I didn't care.

I kept fighting him, started fighting hard, swinging my fist and wind milling my feet. I was throwing my feet like I was running on air. Heavy blows from my bare feet were slapping and stomping on his bare chest. Still, all of that did no good.

Every strike, non-effective.

It was like a guppy versus a shark. A mouse fighting an elephant. This was an unfair war. I was a little woman battling a big man. All of those body blows meant absolutely nothing, didn't budge his hard shell more than an inch. In the end, my wild kicking only fueled his aggression.

He pushed my legs apart, leaned in close to my face. Nose to nose, he growled at me. "So you wanna play rough huh!"

I was terrified but I wouldn't back down. I screamed in his face, kicked and wrestled, tried to bite his face through his mask.

He raised up, grabbed my ankles and threw them straight up into the air.

He said, "So you still wanna fight! I like that! I love a little woman with a lot of fight!" and then he pinned my legs backward.

Toes touching my headboard, my knees at my nose. He folded the life out of me, I had run out of steam. I had no more fight in me and so I figured this was the end.

Folded in two I was defeated and deflated, so I did what any loser would do. I apologized to him.

Outmatched. I told him I wouldn't try anything like that again. Winded. I had no choice other than to fully cooperate.

All of the how-to-survive reality show tactics and feminine crying, humanizing myself and then fighting back, all of it had abandoned my mind.

He raised his chin and looked down at me, cleared his throat and said two words: don't move.

I gripped the sheets, closed my eyes, held my breath and steadied myself. In that order, I prepared myself for a universe of loss and then a split second later his heavy revenge was inside of me again. He was riding deep within my privacy, searching through my personal ecstasy, looking for my g-spot. I could tell by the way he was probing that he was aiming for something, digging for that pleasure chest, looking for me to spill diamonds and gold.

I turned my head to the left, craned my face toward my husband's side of the bed. I inhaled deeply, tried desperately to pick up my husband's scent. I captured his personal fragrance, and in an instance, a picture of my husband's handsome face floated through my brain.

He repeated those two words, "Don't... Move." But when he said it that time, his tone carried a different mood. Those same two words, precise but not quite exact.

His breathing softened. He said, "Please don't... don't move..." my mind said to relax but my body refused to listen. He moaned, separated my legs into a capitol V, and then he gently glided in and out of me.

My thief in the night shook his head slowly, in a sudden change, his voice started pleading, "Please stop moving...please...stop squirming," his movements careful, words expressed gingerly. –There was a subtle moment in time when savage turned tame. And it had nothing to do with conscious persuasion or accidental gratification, but was fully controlled by subconscious gravity- He freed my ankles and then my knees folded into a familiar submission.

He raised the ski mask just above his lips and said, "You're so beautiful," and then he leaned in for another kiss. His lips brushing mine as he whispered, "Just let me... just let go and let me..." and in that moment, starting with my hands, I stopped gripping the sheets and brought my hands up to his half masked face. I tried to touch him but then he leaned back, wouldn't let my hands touch his face.

Looking down at me, his lips curled into a lusty smile. He said, "Tell me you like it baby. Tell me how good this feels to you." His gentle strokes were stirring, mixing and confusing my thoughts.

He inhaled deeply, licked his lips and whispered, "You're so perfect... so angelic." His poetic words and body language was tranquilizing. He gave me insatiable strokes and sensual groans, and then finally, in return, I gave him what a respectable woman shouldn't. I gave him guilty moans.

My response, filled with indistinctive words, yet he understood my tone.

He moved with gratitude and aggression, started tugging my hair. He pulled my head back, and then buried his tongue and teeth into the side of my neck. I had never felt so much energy in my life and I didn't know what to do with all of it. He was pushing me, insisting, moving me in the direction of a place that I had no idea existed. All of this was doing something very strange to me, forcing me to do what I vowed never to do, to unveil what was matrimonial, to tell him things that only my husband had known.

His body relaxing, his movements became fluid. My cooperating had successfully found his hidden weakness.

My devotional moans were long and winding. One after the other, my moans grew stronger. Eyes rolling inside my head, I whispered orgasmic words to myself... please, don't stop.

My guilty conscious held hands with self respect, made me keep that adulterous request to myself.

My fingers crawled to the center of his back, traced up and down his strong spine, drew soft circles on his upper back. With each sweeping loop his body reacted. Under the direction of my invisible puppet string, his hips followed my finger's gentle command.

That touch to his skin was sensual, led him to believe that I was okay with him, to feel like I was making sweet love to him.

And I must confess... I was.

My game of psychological warfare had come to a screeching halt when I stopped pretending that I liked it a few moans ago.

I was giving him what he wanted and had started accepting what I needed, the taboo and the thrill of diabolical sex.

I was audaciously enjoying every inch of my intruder, of the shadowy figure who was taking what exclusively belonged to my lawfully wedded groom.

He kissed me again. I kissed him back.

His body intense, focused, commanding. My body harmonizing, fulfilled, and consenting. His moans were primal and fierce. My moans were as spiritual as rain. He trembled, stiffened. My vaginal walls contracting against his heat. Oh God... Oh God... I can't believe this is happening. Pulling, fighting, struggling against all that was forbidden, I surrendered to unspoken desires and embraced my own voluptuous orgasm as he poured his warm liquid deep inside of me.

I let go, felt incredibly free. And I did it with pleasure because of what he had just given to me: The experience of doing what was wrong. The satisfaction of fucking a stranger in the middle of the night, of being dominated by a man who recognized the sexual effervescence that had been bottled up inside of me.

Exhausted, our roles had reversed. He was now the vulnerable one. Lying there, he was breathless and still.

I took that moment to seize the opportunity.

I eased the rest of his mask away from his relaxed head, wanted to be able to identify this man, to see his face completely.

I slid it away and then studied him.

The side of his face was resting between my breast, his handsome face was painted with innocence and peace.

I ran my fingers through his soft hair, and then I kissed him on his forehead.

My kiss raised his eyes to mine.

We locked gazes for a long moment and then I nudged him.

I gestured for him to get off of me.

He asked me if I had enjoyed it.

I told him that goes without being said. Now it was time for me to pose a question to him.

I asked, "What can I expect the next time a stranger seduces me."

My husband's only reply, "You'll just have to wait and see."

What happened that night was more than scandalous. In fact, the best way that I can describe it is: Sinfullicious.

SHADOWY FIGURE REFLECTION...

This story was at the request of a reader who felt that their marriage was lacking thrill and excitement. I decided to write this in honor of all of the dying relationships around the world. "A little role play works wonders when it comes to foreplay."

TWO OF KIND

"Their names were Aphrodisiac and Nymphomaniac. The pair of them as beautiful as the meanings of their names. Their psychoactive powers aroused me beyond measure, while the blend of their female pheromones took me on travels beyond the gates of paradise..."- Angelic Artiaga

FRESH BLACKBERRIES

I TIPPED THE CHAUFFER with a crisp one-hundred-dollar bill just before she pulled away from the dock. I had been on several cruises in the past, but this one was different. I was alone. I was excited.

No date, no girlfriend, no wannabe-girlfriend, no human luggage, and for the first time in a long time; no wife. Finally, I was under no obligation to add salt to the sea.

What I was feeling could be summed up in one word: Freedom.

For this cruise I could be whoever I wanted to be; Jason, Kenneth, Jonathan, hell, maybe even Victor. I was newly single and on a cruise of endless possibilities, so therefore, my real name was of little importance.

The person wearing my white linen pantsuit, Havana Stetson hat, Gucci sunglasses, and carrying the vintage luggage to match was part me, part my alter ego, and the combination of one hell of a good looking young man ready for some serious fun and new adventures.

The weather was great. The summertime star was high in the sky, fondling beautiful bodies dressed in bikinis and sundresses. Shining on the brows of several men sporting Bermuda and Hawaiian style swim trunks roaming the ship's boarding deck; some of them married, some of them not. All of them doing exactly what I was doing; trying to make eye contact with their sexual fantasies.

After listening to the usual safety rules, I headed to my cabin and unpacked my clothes and stow away liquor; a pint of burbon.

Cabin was nice, and small. Travel agent lied.

I disconnected from my electronic leash, put it in my cabin safe and then took a stroll out to the deck in search for a bar. The crowd was thick, island music in the air, everyone ready to set sail and party.

Close to the pool, I sat at the bar, looked at a menu of tropical drinks.

The woman tending the bar was gorgeous. I could tell that she had migrated to America from somewhere in the Middle East, her dark hair and olive skin announcing -what I imagined to be- Persian, or maybe even an Egyptian bloodline. Her hot-pink tube top was snug, black letters Bon Voyage connecting her small breasts. Her toned arms and sun-kissed shoulders were smooth, I wanted reach across the bar and touch her skin.

Her wild curly hair framing her beautiful face, she smiled at me. "What can I get for you?" her tone, flirtatious.

My eyes traced those letters across her chest again; I mouthed the two words, "Bon Voyage", and then glanced up to her soft face. She was so pretty, made me feel uneasy.

"Uh…" I chucked, cleared my throat, stared down at the menu, "Let's see… It's early, so how about something mild, something easy." I said that with a one-sided smile.

I gave my eyes to her lips, she smiled back at me.

She said, "Good journey."

"Is good journey made with rum?"

Resting on her elbows she leaned into me, whispered, "Bon voyage means good journey."

She grazed the back of my hand with a finger, giggled.

Her soft touch eased me out of my trance, pulled my eyes away from her glossy lips and sent them up to hers.

I had been busted, daydreaming about nasty shit I wanted her to do with her shiny lips.

I played it off with a laugh.

Her smile broadened, and for a brief moment, we held that eye contact.

In that moment I realized she had green eyes peppered with tiny gold specs. She was intoxicating.

I ran my hand down my goatee, inhaled and swallowed. "Okay. Well, how about this. Why don't you just mix me up something you think I'd like?"

She giggled again, slid the menu from my hand, and placed it in the hand of a new passenger.

Sitting there at the bar, unable to get rid of my stupid grin, I watched as she turned and worked her magic.

She picked up a bottle of Red Label Vodka, triple sec, and lime juice and started mixing. Her small breast jiggling as she vigorously shook the vodka, sec, and lime juice together in a silver tumbler before pouring it into an hourglass shaped, lime green plastic cup that had been decorated with tropical flowers.

More vacationers crowded the bar as she put her finishing touches on my special drink. She handed me the colorful cup topped with a pineapple wedge and tiny umbrella.

"Kamikazi." Her lips smiled at me again.

I thanked her with a small head nod and reached for my front shirt pocket, I wanted to tip her before she moved on to the other thirsty passengers; but before I could pull out the bills, a voluptuous cleavage walked over to the bar.

Standing only a few inches from me, was the scent of fresh fruit and flowers. I could smell her. Her scent so alive, I could almost taste her. She smelled and looked amazing. Another beauty from somewhere in the East. Only she looked like she was also blended with a little of something extra from America. African American, or perhaps American Indian.

Tall, slender but curvaceous, everything that would keep a man satisfied. She had full lips and almond eyes, a glowing complexion and soft wavy hair. Her DNA blend was one of a kind; majestic and rare. She was a perfect ten and my perfect fantasy.

I relaxed my shoulders. She stepped closer to me. Her erotic eyes caressing my face like I was the most handsome man in the world.

Without breaking her gaze, she moaned a few words to the bartender, "Please. Allow me."

21

Her voice was sultry; under the influence of sex. Her posture, intimidating. Eyes, lurking. Her aura was powerful, molesting every inch of me.

She winked her long dark lashes at the bartender then slid fifty-dollar-bill across the bar. The Bartender picked it up, smiled while tucking it into her back pocket.

Beautiful and a big tipper.

The Big Tipper eyed me again for a brief moment, blew me a quiet kiss, and then casually eased away.

Steel drums playing Calypso music and the hum of happy chatter evaporating into the wild blue sky, I watched her tiny waist and string bikini snake through the crowd.

Just like that, she had me.

Just like that, I wanted to be had.

I raised a brow, looked left and right. Tried reading the faces of the barflies standing around waiting for drinks, wondered if they were seeing what I was seeing.

Breath caught in my throat, I glanced back toward the Bartender. She was serving a new passenger an umbrella-covered drink. But then she turned to me, gave me a thin smile as she cupped her hands and ran them down the curves of her round behind.

Looking at her, caught in a trance, my breathing became shallow. It had only been a few minutes since the ship had set sail and already the tides had started to change. I wasn't expecting to be hunted but I was definitely ready for their chase.

She dropped her eyes to my lips, and then slowly licked hers. Her tongue gliding from left to right, moving in slow motion, and that did something strange to me. Like licking an envelope, that gesture had captured me, sealed some sort of a deal. These two women had worked together, had tag-teamed and set things in motion for catching their prey. In that moment I suddenly realized that not only was I being hunted, but ultimately, I was going to be their kill.

The rules in the game of chase had changed, and I was speechless.

A direct message had just been sent between the women, a provocative message that I had overheard, a form communication sent in an encrypted sign language with the complexities of Morse code.

Neither woman had uttered a single syllable to me, but their body language was loud and clear.

The Bartender turned her back to me and I took in the entire view of what she was offering up for me to see. She was mouthwatering.

I shook my head, swallowed hard, and turned away from her, scanned the deck searching for the sexy Big Tipper, but she had vanished into the flood of vacationers.

The Bartender continued serving up drinks to more cruisers. Her smile was bright and professional. She had turned her attention completely away from me. It was as if I'd become invisible and all of what had just happened was just my imagination and not really what it seemed.

I decided to move away from the bar, drifted over to the pool area. I relaxed into a poolside recliner; people watched and enjoyed my drink.

After sitting there for a few minutes, I fell into a deep daze.

I couldn't stop thinking about the subtle but explicit come-ons from the two women.

I wasn't tripping.

What had just happened was real, and was not just my twisted imagination.

I felt their heavy pursuit, and I liked it.

But then again I felt anxious, wondered if that was how women were made to feel.

I'd never experienced anything quite like that before.

Those two incredible women churned my thoughts; their images wouldn't leave my head. Made me feel a strong tingle, an electric surge moving from the head of my lingam to the center of my chest. Made my partner in crime swell, get excited, want to come out and get a bird's eye view of what I had just seen.

I started talking to him, called him by his name: Harold. My ex-wife had named him Harold, and it stuck.

I pressed the heel of my palm down on my zipper, told Harold to be cool, told him we had seven whole days left to be on this ship, that he had plenty of time to come out to play.

I sipped my drink, and before long the sun started crossing the intersection between Earth and sky, so I decided to head back to my cabin to get ready for some nighttime fun.

As I approached my stateroom, I noticed a small pink card wedged in my cabin door.

I looked around.

There was no one in sight.

I snatched it out of the door jam, focused on the feminine handwriting.

It read: 'If you love big tippers, meet me near the bar at The Black Mango. Tonight!'

I scanned the card twice, thought I'd read: 'If you love big TITTIES...' And to think; I'm a writer. But in that moment, and after the direct hit placed on me out by the deck's bar; literature was the farthest thing from my mind.

I stared at the words written on the card.

'The Black Mango.'

I'd heard a lot about the nightclub. It was one of the biggest selling points in the ship's brochure. Images of beautiful women, a live DJ, liquor.

'Damn!'

I wanted to go.

I needed to go.

I pushed my cabin key-card in the slot, waited for the little green light. I stepped inside, closed the door behind me and then flopped down on the side of my small bed. I smiled to myself, shook my head. "This is wild."I reached over, grabbed the bottle of bourbon by the neck and poured myself a drink. No ice. No frills. I needed something strong, something with smooth heat.

I threw it back, flipped on the cabin's SIRIUS radio, Kirk Whalum's Anytime sailed into my small space, took me on another vacation.

I kicked up my feet, relaxed before heading out for the night.

I was a newly single man, had been newly hunted, and was now tempted to enter the trap.

Seduced by beautiful strangers—two women I wanted to fuck, two women I hoped wanted to fuck me.

Half hour later I got up. Showered. Shaved away the shadow that'd joined me at five o'clock. Got dressed. A black button up and slacks, black Maddens loafers, silk socks.

I did a once-over in the mirror before I walked out the door. My line up was tight and I was ready for whatever.

Happy Caribbean music paced my leather footsteps through the carpeted hall, down the escalator and into the sound of R&B coming through the double-doors of The Black Mango.

I took a deep breath and stepped into the club. The DJ was live, bobbing his head and encouraging the crowd through his microphone. Everybody was partying like crazy. The orgasmic dance floor was full of vacationers waving half-full shot glasses in the air. Dancing lip gloss, perfume and men's cologne. A hundred orgies in the making. Their sexual excitement painted with The Black Mango's laser light show, lights that also danced to the heavy bass coming through the speakers.

I looked over toward the bar and that's when I locked eyes with the lip-licking Bartender. She was pouring liquid courage from two slim bottles held high above her head. Her hair was wild and curly, decorated with stones that shinned like diamonds. She poured and overflowed a row of seven shot glasses lined up on the bar. All eyes on her, she was more than a bartender, she was an entertainer.

Time slowed. Sound moaned.

Dancing bodies starting to sway like underwater swimmers. Heartbeat drumming in my ears, palms breaking into a sweat, everyone fading into a dark shadow as an imaginary spotlight settled on the Big Tipper's voluptuous cleavage.

There she was, sitting on the edge of a barstool waiting for me. Clear stilettos exposing her bare feet and red toe nails.

Smooth calves, toned thighs, and a short red dress hugging her body; the perfect complement to her red lips pulled into a wicked smile. Her soft waves were lifted off her neck, a white Plumeria - the tropical lei flower with white petals and a golden center- pinned behind her right ear.

Time and sound returned to live speed, and so did I. I popped in an Altoid and resumed my pace. I moved toward the bar.

I approached the beautiful Big Tipper, cleared my throat, formally introduced myself.

Blurting over the loud music. "I'm Harold..." I shook my head fast, "I mean Terrance!"

BOOM! Party foul! I wanted to kill myself.

She giggled at my nervousness.

I chewed my Altoid, ran my sweaty palms down the sides of my pant legs and then reached for her hand, wanted to give her a gentle handshake. But instead of shaking my hand, she lifted it to her face, sucked my middle finger into her warm mouth.

Oh Shit!

Her strong tongue rolled my finger, moved to the beat of R&B, a combination that made my thighs twitch and Harold's head press hard against my zipper.

I didn't want to be rude so I let her have her way, didn't pull my finger away from her lips.

I licked my lips, the Big Tipper stopped sucking and stood up in front of me. She put her soft cheek against mine and whispered into my ear, "Harold... Terrance. You do remember your liquor from earlier?" She leaned away from me and threw her eyes toward the one who was obviously her co-conspirator.

My eyes followed hers, went to the sexy drink server she'd so generously tipped earlier. "Absolutely. Is she your friend?" My question rhetorical.

"You can say that."

The music changed, a slower tempo, gave everybody the opportunity to switch partners, sit down, crowd the bar.

She eased her soft behind back onto the barstool, adjusted

26

herself and poetically crossed her thighs.

Sharon Stone.

Her body language was tranquilizing.

She asked, "Did you enjoy your drink?"

My gaze found her cleavage and then crawled up to her red lips. "Yes…yes I did."

"Do you want another one?"

She was so fucking sexy.

I handed her an absorbing stare, told her, "I don't want to be greedy."I tilted my head slightly, was giving sexy back. Two can play that game.

"Oh, but you should be..." A Cheshire cat, she purred, "Grrreedy."

She uncrossed and then seductively crossed her soft legs in the opposite direction, pointed her red toes toward the sexy Bartender. Another message; sent and received.

I said, "You think so?"

"Oh yes I do… In fact…" She reached up, touched my lips with two fingers. "I think you should have…two, this time." Her eyes squinting, a red devilish smile crawling across her pretty face.

"Two?" I raised a brow.

She nodded.

She was precise, knew exactly what she wanted, exactly how to ask for it.

I wasn't expecting so much so soon.

Breathing tight, heart galloping in my chest, and now Harold really putting up a fight.

She stood up, leaned into me, her breath warm on my ear, she whispered those magic words, "Take me to your room."

I took an easy step back, looked into her eyes.

The music was loud, I wasn't sure if I had heard what I hoped I had heard.

She took an easier step close to me, pressed her body against mine, slid one hand down and around my ass, palmed and stroked my crotch with the other, sent my mind into warp drive.

'Damn she's bold.'

Harold got hard.

I got weak.

My legs felt like they were about to buckle underneath me.

She moved her lips toward mine. I started relaxing mine apart. My tongue expected a juicy kiss, but she whispered into my opened mouth instead. She said, "Take me to your room. Take me right now." Her request was loud and clear that time, left no room for error.

I chuckled, ran my hand down my goatee. I looked around the club, chuckled some more, wondered if this was some type of a joke. I had always dreamed of having a night like this, but never thought it would ever actually happen.

I played it cool, composed myself, and then gladly took the bait.

I said, "Right this way." Abracadabra, her wish was my command. If she was game, I wanted to play.

She looked over to the Bartender, gave her the same slow wink she had given her earlier. The Bartender laughed under her breath, blew me her familiar kiss.

I caught it. Bait swallowed.

I had been hooked and now they were reeling me in.

I held the Big Tipper's soft hand, lead her out of R&B and into a new Caribbean swing, up the elevator and toward the narrow door of my stateroom.

On our travel to my room, we were silent. There hadn't been two words exchanged between us. All the talking had been done inside my head. 'Just be cool…enjoy the ride.'

We approached my cabin, I bent my eyes down to her, my gaze traveled south of her pretty face, stopped, was trained on her swollen breasts, on her ripe nipples pressing hard against her red dress. Imprints of beautiful round rubies. I imagined my tongue flickering across those rubies, my hand caressing her soft, wet center.

I used my cabin key card and swung open the door. The SIRIUS radio was still on low, softly painting the room with a

28

different color of smooth jazz.

No hesitation.

She slid out of her red dress and made herself comfortable on my bed.

My crotch her focal point, she let her hair down and slid her palms across the bed spread. Her soft waves fell down to her shoulders, I was transfixed.

I let go of the door and walked over to her, wanted to touch her hair.

I stood in front of her nudity, her flesh perfect, not wearing a single blemish. My knees against the bed, wedged between her pretty legs. Her eyes smoldering, looking up at me, saying things that were X-Rated. Towering over her, we became beauty and the beast, or Samson and Delilah. I was much bigger, much stronger. But in that moment, got lost in her eyes, became weak, right then she had complete control over me.

She eased her focus back to what was eye level, to what stood inches in front of her face, and then put her mouth on my crotch. She started tonguing and nudging Harold through the fabric of my slacks and that paralyzed me. I pulled in a heavy breath, let my head fall back.

Harold started jumping, throbbing, and drooling pre-cum. He was anxious, wanted to be freed.

In frenzy, she unzipped my pants and Harold flopped out. The sight of him, of his size, paused her. Her hands started out moving fast, but the significance of him slowed her down. She raised her eyes to mine, flared her narrow nostrils and then licked her lips. She opened her mouth wide and stuck out her tongue. I was the doctor, and Harold was a tongue suppresser.

She was ready, and I was ready too.

I could see the little punching bag hanging at the back of her throat, and I wanted to hit it hard.

I tangled my fingers in her hair and guided her head backward. I steadied myself, slid Harold across her hot tongue. I shivered as I eased him into the back of her throat, to where he settled nicely between her tonsils. Her face relaxed, she pulled him even deeper into her throat, held that position, suckled with smooth control. I listened as she moaned, as she swallowed him whole. I almost lost it as she painted multicolored fantasies with her talented tongue.

Thrusting forward I gripped her hair tight and gave her exactly what she wanted.

I watched her red lips stretch around and hug my hard dick. I whispered, "Fuck yeah..."

A new face giving me oral sex was an old fantasy being fulfilled.

I moved my hands from her hair, gently caressed her chin, fed her, guided her head back, and forth. Mouth open, I stared at her performance, watched Harold disappear and then reappear out past her red lips. She was amazing, working my chocolate pole like a pro. Eyes rolling, I threw my head back, thanked the universe for gifting her, for making this sexy shit happen to me.

I reached down, squeezed her breast, pinched her nipple. Her skin felt sticky and smelled sweet.

With a long and tight suck she pulled her head all the way back, the tip of her pink tongue waving goodbye to Harold.

She stood on the bed, held onto my shoulders, leaned over and feathered her nipples against my lips. I stuck out my tounge, tasted them.

She had creamed her body with something edible, something that had made her feel, smell, and now taste sticky-sweet.

The temperature in the room got hot, went from a mild 74 to what felt like 150 degrees, a heat sending fat beads of sweat rolling down the back of my neck.

Head moving fast, going back and forth, tongue jumping from one nipple to the other; I palmed, sucked, and licked both of her beautiful breasts. Breathing heavy, in another world—I felt crazed, heady.

The sound of smooth jazz from the SIRUS radio changed. Became blended with bongos, tambourines, and six string guitar. The medley of Caribbean dreams playing in the hall was now seeping into my room.

Preoccupied with the Big Tipper, I didn't turn around to inspect the sound.

Out of nowhere I felt a slight breeze cascading across the back of my damp neck. Its coolness carrying a new and intoxicating scent, an aroma of bold femininity. I inhaled deep. Stroked the Big Tipper's body. Gave her soft kisses.

And then as suddenly as it had come, the Caribbean music was cut off.

The sounds of the islands abruptly died, but the new scent was still alive.

I found myself surrounded by a bouquet of wild sex.

It was stimulating, controlling me.

It come into my cabin bearing new gifts, escorting a second pair of soft lips, a new set fluffy pillows had come in and joined us at the bed.

Like being touched by an angel, a soft hand slid around my right thigh, and then that's when I felt it. Puffs of warmth tapping against me.

I heard a soft voice whisper hello, and then a breath later I felt it; the most incredible sensation know to man; another hot wet blanket gradually wrapping around the head of my dick.

I shook my head in disbelief.

This shit is fucking unreal...

Eyes closed tight, I didn't want to look down, refused to wake from this vivid dream.

Harold was being licked, nibbled, and swallowed sideways by a phantom mouth.

In that moment, being a man became so hard. And being pleased by two by two goddesses doing everything a man could dream of; made being a man so fucking hard.

I struggled, ached, willed myself not to lose control. It all felt so legendary; feeling, tasting, and hearing moaning songs of two sexy sirens was music to my ears.

I savored the moment.

Tasted one woman while the other tasted me.

31

I ran my tongue down the cleavage of one and directed the fast and slow paces of the other.

My tongue moved down the Big Tippers stomach, around her belly button, and between her thighs. I traveled south toward my destination and didn't stop until I found her aphrodisiac.

I grazed the slippery slit of the Big Tipper. Her river so sweet it brought me to my knees.

I eased to the floor, and like a baby giraffe suckling from its mother, without interruption, the hot mouth sucking my dick craned its neck and followed.

Eyes locked shut, I fell further into the mystery mouth's groove. Her slow and deliberate sucks making my toes curl, my head spin.

Tasting milk chocolate and fresh blackberries on the Big Tipper, and being tasted by what had to be a nymphomaniac at the same time, was a nuptial I would never want to divorce.

I was eating one and feeding the other, and then my fingers moved between new legs, broke the seal on our hungry guests.

Fingers sliding in and out of silky wetness dripping from the newcomer, was a provocative nuptial I would never want to divorce.

"Look at me," The Big Tipper moaned, "Feed your eyes baby. Enjoy what you're eating." She palmed the back of my head, "Look at me baby... open your eyes... look at this pussy." She was grinding against my goatee.

Her wish was my command.

I opened one eye, looked at her hairless pussy. It was pretty. Deserving of being on display, placed on a pedestal next to the world's most prized possessions. She was a work of art, as magnificent as the sculpture by Alexandrous of Antionch; the Venus de Milo. Only she was better.

She was a masterpiece.

Alive.

Covered in warm flesh, a sculpture made from the dust of the Earth, a sculpture crafted by the creator.

The Big Tipper's sweet pink opening stared back at me. There for the taking, it was all for me, and so I lost myself. I closed my eyes and went headlong, gave her slow slurps and deep kisses.

I turned my head sideways, lined those pretty lips with mine. Tongue kissed her like she was my first girlfriend, as if she was my first love, the one every young man wants to impress. I stiffened my tongue, licked her candied clit with a flurry of licks, told her every secret that had been caught in my mind, every thought I'd held captive since adolescence.

This was better than autoeroticism, this was real. This was pouring oil on fire.

I ran my tongue through the Devil's canal while being devoured by the Devil herself.

I was being sucked with strokes of genius, could feel her mouth but still hadn't seen her face.

I eased my hand down, touched her hair.

Big.

Soft and curly.

"Mmmm, you taste so good." A soft moan from down below.

I swallowed raw sugar and tilted my eyes down in the direction of the voice.

Wild hair and a greedy mouth moaning the most eloquent song. It was her, the Big Tipper's trigger man. No longer wearing the words Bon Voyage and tight jeans; she was wearing a spandex black dress.

The Bartender. By my side. Kneeling. Paying homage to me.

Taking all of Harold into her beautiful mouth. She was skilled, moved across Harold's long body effortlessly. In and out of her mouth she was giving award winning philacio, doing it like a professional, without grazing him with her teeth. I wondered if she had been trained by Super Head herself.

Two beautiful strangers pleasuring me was as controversial as the book of Judas.

The Big Tipper had the most incredible body. The Bartender

had the softest lips.

The Big Tipper's eyes were glazed over and locked on me, rubbing her clit with her middle fingertip, she did that without blinking. Bartender rocking me, I watched carefully as the Big Tipper traced small circles around her clit, as her fingers glided up and down between those hairless lips.

This was my wildest dream turned reality, and I was enjoying every moment of it.

The Bartender held an opened bottle of Courvoisier in one hand, and used the other to hot dog Harold far into the back of her hungry throat.

The fragrance of sex, chocolate, and fresh blackberries rising from the Big Tippers center triggered senses that made me want to come.

Looking down at the Bartender, her jaws tight, giving me full eye contact was pushing me toward the edge. Moaning, slowly sucking my whole dick, pleasing me with her labor of love, alternating between shallow and deep, nose against my belly deep, was magnificent.

I needed to come, I almost did it, could hardly hold it.

But the Bartender felt the subtle vibration of hot blood rising, the heat of my orgasm rushing to the end of my dick. She didn't want the party to stop, so she stopped licking Harold's drooling lips.

The Bartender rose from her knees and then she sat on the edge of the narrow bed, reached over and grabbed my bottle of bourbon.

My eyes followed her, smiled at hers.

I leaned in, gave her a kiss. That put a smile on her face.

She held the bottle of liquor over the Big Tippers stomach, poured it across her sex. I watched as it streamed across her clit and pooled between her swollen lips. I looked at the Bartender and then she licked her lips. She smiled at me again, her eyes telling me to take a sip. She had poured me a rare and exotic drink, one that wasn't on the menu at the bar.

The Big Tipper was squirmed, gyrated, the brown liquor

traveled down through the crack of her ass. I grabbed the back of the Big Tippers thighs, lifted her legs back, and drank from her fleshy cup. Fruit, chocolate, bourbon covered pussy; an elixir the Bartender's tongue also indulged.

Biting her bottom lip, Big Tipper ran her fingers through the Bartender's ringlets of wild hair. Frowning, the Big Tipper gave me a telling stare. The sting of the liquor, the feel of the Bartender's bisexual kisses, was wicked and stirring to her naughty soul.

The Big Tipper moved her gaze toward Harold, ran her tongue across her red lips. She pushed the Bartender's head from between her legs and then she inched over on the bed, made room for her sexy friend.

The Bartender pulled her dress over her wild hair, threw it to the floor.

The Bartender turned the bottle straight up, brown liquid spilling from the corners of her mouth. She took long gulps and then wiped her chin with the back of her hand.

I stood up, was looking down at them. I couldn't believe my fucking eyes. Both of them were looking up at me. And then both women, as if on the count of three, opened their legs simultaneously.

The Bartender, she was hairless too, Brazilian bikini waxed, they looked like Doublemint twins. Two pretty pussies, purring, hissing, puckering, blowing wet kisses at me.

The Big Tipper started patting her throbbing sex with her right hand. Breathing in the state of desperation, eyes locked on Harold, she said, "I want to feel him inside." Still playing with her own clit, she moved her other hand between the Bartender's legs, pushed her middle finger far inside of her, did that like she wanted to hurt her. "And she wants some too."

I shook my head in disbelief. Two squirming bodies twisting in my bed.

I held Harold in the palm of my hand, spoke to him telepathically, told him to choose the one he wanted to get to know first.

Two women, four languages. All of them spoken with fluency.

The Big Tipper whispering into the air, her words inaudible like an album spun backward. The Bartender was moaning, pain in her brow, her tone more aggressive, almost pleading. Voiceless words coming from their unchartered paradises, my tropical destination living between their legs.

All sounds hypnotizing. Their erotic symphony an arrangement of seductive notes.

The Big Tipper was moving, gyrating, pinching her nipples, calling out to me.

The Bartender touched herself, poured bourbon over her own pink opening, mixed a new drink for me.

My head spun. Harold's head throbbed with anxiety. I massaged my temple with one hand, stroked Harold's tension away with the other.

Tensed and confused, I wanted to kiss both of them. Tense and thrilled, Harold wanted to fuck both of them.

I reached into my overnight bag, rolled on a condom, and further without debate Harold went for the Big Tipper, tunneled deep inside of her. My body rocked, under her control as my eyes drifted to the Bartender's liquored lips; went from the lips on her pretty face to the lips between her pretty legs.

While Harold was fucking the Big Tipper, touching her g-spot over and over again, giving her an orgasmic thrill, pulling her toward the brink of insanity, I gazed deeply at the Bartender's everything.

A long moment of staring back at me, the Bartender eventually said, "Come fuck me too... I want some of that dick too." And then she leaned forward and slid her soft hand under my balls.

The way she said that, how she cradled my heat, I felt it was my duty to give her exactly what she wanted.

She started licking and sucking her lips again, her long tongue sweeping the Big Tipper's elixir from the corners of her mouth. The way the Bartender kept looking at me, she had ferociousness in her green-and-gold eyes, one that spoke violently to me, that drove me mad, took me to the next level. I grabbed her by her wild hair and tasted her lips, enjoyed the sweetness of the Big Tipper with the Bartender's deep kiss.

I wanted to kiss the Bartender's sun kissed face from the first moment I saw her, from the moment she first looked at me. Now I was getting more than a sweet kiss, now I was kissing her with untamed lust.

Both women moaning. Me groaning. Their resonance punishing me, dragging me to the land of what-the-fuck!

I wanted to come, but moved the thought out of my head. I didn't want to be a ten-minute lover.

Harold and I switched.

He slid down The Bartender's slippery slope. I watched as he broke through her lips, as I pushed him deep inside of the only thing that mattered, and within a few seconds, I was ready to come again. Her pussy was just as tight, but wetter than the Big Tipper's.

Maybe it was the anticipation from all day, maybe it wasn't. The one thing that I can testify to is that from the moment I eased down inside, it was on. The Bartender instantly struck orgasmic fires, sent them running up my thighs. Harold was cocked and loaded, an ignited cannon ready to explode.

They moaned and groaned. I groaned and moaned.

I was about to come, there was no turning back this time. The Bartender was working the hell out of me. Squeezing and pulling, showing off her Kegel skills, giving me no other choice.

The Big Tipper sucked my tongue into her mouth, said unladylike and vulgar words. Told me to fuck the shit out of the Bartender, to fuck her long and hard. She told me to make the Bartender scream and for me to make her pussy cry painful tears.

I couldn't take it. They were driving me to the island of insanity.

I pulled Harold out of The Bartender, took control of him. I pulled off the condom and rubbed and stroked him good and fast.

Both women clawing at me, mouths open toward the ceiling, little birds begging to be fed.

Harold expanded, veins traveling the hard distance of his length. He was single-minded, strong.

Eyes zigzagging between the women, at their faces, their mouths, between their soft legs. I became aggressive and so I aggressively stroked.

The Bartender and the Big Tipper begged and moaned in a hypnotizing harmony; casting a spell over me, a spell over Harold.

Harold refused to hold back.

Every muscle strained. Teeth tight, jaws clenched, sweat crawling across my brow, I was concentrating, staring at feral sex.

Harold exploded like fireworks.

Showered their faces with a wild spray of silver and gold.

It was The Magic Kingdom's nighttime spectacular, the place where all of my dreams came true.

They latched onto Harold, wrestled over who was going to suck what was left in him, who was going to swallow his sugary sap first.

They held, licked, and sucked Harold clean. They caressed my balls, the source of their nectar, and then nibbled at them like juicy plums, the forbidden fruit growing in the Garden of my Eden. When Harold had nothing left to spill, my legs went weak and I stumbled backward. I watched those two talented tongues dance together in celebration, kissing and exchanging what Harold had given them.

On the floor, next to the bed, they had brought me to my knees again.

Everything fading in and out, ears ringing, my vision blurred.

On my back, still and helpless, I watched the two foggy silhouettes leave...

"Good morning passengers, this is your captain speaking from the bridge..." The early morning PA announcement was my alarm clock.

I had passed out and woke up with my pants down around my ankles.

Groggy, I looked up at the ceiling, and then remembered where I was. I wondered if I had awakened from a dream.

I sat up, looked around, reached down for my pants.

And there it was.

The plumeria flower; my empty bourbon bottle its vase.

I took the tropical flower from the bottle's mouth, rubbed its soft petals against my nose.

Fresh blackberries, chocolate, liquor, and a fragrance called sex.

Evidence of reality.

Last night was not a dream and had actually ridden two escalators to heaven.

My vacation itinerary was for seven days.

And that was only day one.

FRESH BLACKBERRIES REFLECTION...

This story was originally written for one of my readers named Harold who wrote in to me and said, "Angelic, I would love to see myself in a sexy position on vacation." I instantly thought, 'cruise & two beautiful women'. After writing his story, I emailed it to him. He was very excited, and needless to say... wanted to go on a cruise. Thanks Harold!

THE TRUTH

"I can remember you told me to lie still, whispered, "Spread your legs", you told me to let you see if you can find it. By stroke number three... my G-spot was detonated, and I exploded over and over again. It was the moment of truth. The moment I admitted, "You are the TRUTH."
- Angelic Artiaga

THE WINE STACKER

"SNIFFING PUSSY willows and the scent of chestnut trees breezing through my front window had taken its toll on me. I was completely sick of the artificial smells of jism they sprayed into my small house, and was ready to inhale the real thing..."

It had been almost a year since Michael and I started working for the same California winery, six months since we'd last seen each other, and three days since he'd finally popped the question and asked me out on our first date; a date that was completely against company policy; so it goes without being said that our plans made me feel a little nervous.

He was based at the actual vineyard and I traveled from one major distribution retailer to another. Overseeing the winemaking process was his job, while sealing deals and creating new accounts was mine.

It was a beautiful September afternoon in Wine Country, the time of year that puts wineries in full swing, and so therefore, I left home early for our date.

The Napa Valley traffic was littered with a crush tourist, most of them Europeans who were either going too fast or too slow as they adjusted to driving left-steering American cars.

Overestimating the weight of traffic, I arrived to our meeting location – our winery of all places- about twenty minutes too early. There was a pretty big event going on that day, so the parking lot was packed with rented cars, SUV's, and foreigners enjoying the perfect 76 degree weather.

I freshened up my lip gloss, grabbed my little beaded purse, and stepped out of my silver Prius.

My reflection in the driver's-side window was quite lovely.

Wearing a buttery yellow, my dress was simple, yet inviting; a halter, perfect for a first date.

Not only did I look pretty, but I felt pretty.

Walking through the parking lot, I smiled at my soft yellow chiffon as it waved in the summer wind. And with each wave I grew more and more excited about our evening of wine tasting.

I moved with the other visitors past beautiful landscaping as we made our way over to the grape groves, our noses lead by the earthy scent of irrigation marinating the vine roots where little humming birds flitted from blossom to blossom, their tiny wings beckoning us to walk through the groves.

At the mouth of the groves, there sat a short chubby Italian gentleman dressed like a Gondolier.

He was costumed in fifteenth century clothing; black slacks, black and white striped shirt with red sashes tied around his waist and brim of a woven straw hat. Strumming a mandolin and serenading the visitors with a cheery Italian song, his walrus mustache greeted me with a welcoming smile as I bounced past him and nodded hello.

When I finally reached the winery's tall studded front doors, I stalled but then took a moment and encouraged myself. Here we go.

I pulled the door open and walked into an atmosphere of excitement; there were hundreds of faces that I had never seen. Instantly my concerns were at ease.

With all of that excitement in the air, and since our winery employed a few thousand people who hardly mingled together, I figured going unrecognized amongst the sea of faces should be a breeze.

I relaxed my arms down at my sided and casually strolled over to an open spot at the winery's reception bar where I wedged myself between tasters. I grabbed the attention of a hostess, asked her for a glass of Rosé and then glanced around the large room. The interior of the winery was spectacular.

Being a field rep, I had only visited the winery a couple times, and from what I remembered, looking around, I couldn't help but notice that the winery had undergone a serious facelift. Totally renovated with opulence. New carpeted floors and mahogany paneled walls adorned with vintage paintings framed in gold trimmings. A built in surround sound entertaining the tasters with the sounds of Italy. Impressive. Expensive.

Standing at the bar I noticed a grandfather clock hanging adjacent to the bar. I read the time; a quarter to six.

"A glass of Rose." The hostess smiled.

I thanked her and then was hit with a new set nervousness. In that moment I remembered the risk in dating a co-worker, our company's very strict policy against that.

My palms began to sweat and my brain wondered if I should reconsider this. I think should just go back to my car, and leave.

I pulled my phone from my purse, was about to give him a call, cancel our date, but when I tapped the screen there was a text waiting for me:

FROM: MIKE "See you in a minute. I'm really looking forward to spending some time with you."

It was too late to leave, too late to stop this train. So I slid my phone back into my purse and readied myself for this date.

Holding the stem, a soft tulip between my fingertips, I looked down into my glass of pink summer. I inhaled its luscious blend of femininity; its sweet scent as lovely as Valentine's Day. 'Relax. This is going to be great.'

Just as I put the glass to my lips, a nice-looking man squeezed into the small space between me and a woman standing less than a foot away from me. The space was so tight that his hand slowly grazed across my thigh.

I felt it.

His touch was so... I don't know...On purpose.

So I set the glass down, perfected my posture, and said, "I didn't see you walk in." Smiling coolly, I turned and laid my eyes on him.

He turned to me, and for a brief moment he stared vacantly before handing me an 'Oh-really' smile.

An awkward moment was born, and I wanted to die.

I locked eyes with him, cleared my throat. "Oh… oh my goodness… I'm sorry… I…" I felt so silly. But he had moved in so close, hand on my thigh, I automatically assumed he was my date. Well…he wasn't.

He chuckled, shook his head. "No worries." He reached across his chest to shake my hand, "And by the way, my name is…" But before he could say his name; flushed and embarrassed; as I went for his hand I clumsily tipped over my glass of Rosé!

I yelped, "Oh Shit!" and tried hopping from my seat.

Stool rocking backward, he caught me before I hit the floor. I took hold of his arm and braced myself. He helped me from the stool and steadied me onto my feet.

His eyes grew large. "Are you okay?"

"Oh my Gosh!" I inspected his white shirt, his creamy pants; no Rosé. Shaking my head fast. "I am so sorry!"

He felt bad. "No. I apologize… I must have startled you." His eyes scaled the front of my dress, my eyes did the same. I had jumped back trying to dodge the spill but my leap was too late. The Rose had splashed onto the front of my yellow dress; a big pink stain left in its wake.

I was speechless, embarrassed beyond belief, and like a lunatic just kept shaking my head.

I felt so damn foolish.

All eyes on me.

I stood there looking like an idiot waiting for an applause.

He grabbed a pile of napkins from the bar and I snatched them from him, quickly swiped at the stain spreading across the front of my dress.

He said, "Hold on, let me help you with that." And then grabbed more napkins. He tried dabbling at the rosy spot racing toward the hem of my dress.

Still shaking my head, I insisted. "No. No thank you!" I tried taking the new napkins from his hand, but he held onto them, cautiously touched my shoulder, a gesture made for calming my nerves. He dipped his head beneath mine, looked into my eyes, whispered, "Are you sure?" He flashed me sincere smile. "Honestly, I don't mind helping. After all, it is partially, if not all, my fault."

I dismissed his consolation, fanned out the yellow fabric. "Damn! Look at my dress!"

I waved at the hostess, mouthed the word –napkins. She threw me one finger, her pointing finger, the one that said 'hold on or one minute'; didn't matter, I couldn't do either.

I gave him eye contact. "Listen, I'm very sorry. I mistook you for someone else... and now look at what I've done." I huffed, swiping at the stain again, only making it worse.

He turned to another hostess who happened to be tipping by, her palm doing a balancing act with a round tray filled with wine glasses, asked her if the winery had any seltzer water to help with my dilemma. She lowered her tray to her waist, looked down at my clumsiness and then shook her head with a slow and sympathetic 'No'.

I huffed again. "Don't worry about it! Please excuse me."

I reached for my purse, looked over at the grandfather clock again; it was still a couple minutes before our scheduled rendezvous. I needed to hurry to the ladies room and get cleaned up before Mike showed up.

I thanked my mistake again for his kindness and then searched for the sign pointing me to the nearest ladies room.

I scanned the room, found no directions.

I marched away from the bar, away from him; repeating the words pardon me and excuse me as I pushed through the buzzing crowd.

Finally, a beacon of light.

I saw a sign reading: RESTROOMS.

I stepped swiftly, eyes glued to the ladies room clipart posted on the ladies room door.

I was a few feet away from my refuge, almost there, and that's when I was stopped dead in my tracks by the smiling face of an approaching man. This happy waving man was coming full steam ahead. His grin was weaving and bobbing through the crowd, peaking over the tops of some people's heads and around the sides of others. This guy was tall, dark, and handsome. He was smiling from ear to ear, his excitement moving fast in my direction.

I squinted my eyes. 'Oh Gosh… Is that him?'

I looked down at the mess covering the front of my dress and then back up to him. I stood there, peering at his face through the mob of people.

It had been a while since I had last seen him, and after what had just happened, I wasn't quite ready to trust my judgment.

He seemed familiar but still there was something unrecognizable about the face plowing through the crowd.

His smile, still infectious.

His eyes, tender and calm.

His stride, spirited and energetic.

All that was the same, but there was something more appealing about him, something that the past six months of space didn't announce right away.

As he grew closer, he grew larger. As he grew larger, so did my trust for my judgment. He threw his palm above the crowd, waved his hand. 'Oh God... it's him!'

By the time he was a stone's throw away from me I'd finally figured out what had changed.

I had heard through the grapevine that he had been living at Gold's Gym, and I must say, that the new definition in his exposed forearms quickly turned that rumor into fact.

I looked down at my new design again, made a wish, "Please make me disappear..." I shook my head in disbelief that my luck could be so bad.

Self-conscious about looking like a slob, I got fidgety, started fumbling with my purse. I pulled my cell from my purse, illuminated its screen. The time read five fifty-nine. And before I could blink, five fifty-nine turned into 6 o'clock.

Damn! Right on time.

He was that way. So Precise.

He strolled up close to me, let out a sharp sigh. "There you are." He gave me a soft peck on my cheek, and then traced my face with his brown eyes. He said, "You look, beautiful."

I nodded. "Thanks. You do too. I mean, you look really good, handsome." I kept nodding like I had an unbreakable habit.

And then there was this pregnant pause growing between us.

He said, "Finally."

I inspected his new physique. Started at his belt buckle and then traveled to his face where we exchanged eye contact and then held it.

After a long moment, I blinked and then smiled. "Yes, finally."

My eyes traveled back in the direction from where they had started. I brushed across his strong neck, down his chest, past his zipper, and then his feet.

He was wearing one of my favorite colors; a baby blue button up that looked tailored to fit perfectly against his broad shoulders and muscular arms. He wore black slacks that hung nicely over his long legs, and smooth black Stantoni Quebeck shoes to match his belt.

He was tall and strong, my favorite kind of man.

I'm five foot five and he is about a foot taller than me. He was sturdy and sexy, a clean shaven picture of every woman's insatiable lust.

Working out had not only changed his posture, it also made distinctive changes in his face. Jaw line chiseled like a finely carved statue, nose perfectly symmetrical above soft full lips that ended with a sexy smirk at the corners.

Looking at this beautiful man was distracting, made me forget about my fashion violation. But a blink later that memory came flying back to the front of mind.

I casually placed my small hands over the big stain but that proved to be useless. By now the mess was so wide that it would have taken ten hands and a few magicians to create an illusion good enough to cover it up.

He said, "I'm happy we're finally going to be spending some time together."

Embarrassment returning, I sighed. "Yeah, me too. Me too."

I scanned the long corridor, searched for a gift shop that may have sold dresses.

It had been forever since I had been to our home winery and a lot had changed. There were all sorts of new additions and upgrades to the main building; if only a gift shop selling dresses were one of them.

He asked, "May I?" And then he wrapped his strong arms around me, gave me a warm hug. My nose brushed against his chest, I inhaled him. He smelled so good. As delicious as midnight sex.

That one whiff of masculinity was incredible, persuasive, but not enough to keep me from unlocking our embrace and pulling away from him.

He frowned down at me, his strong jaw clenched with concern, he asked, "Is everything okay?"

I threw my eyes to the ladies room and then back to his. I was at a loss for all words that made any sense of my stupid mistake, so I just shook my head like a fool suffering from a nervous twitch.

He smile was pleading, he asked, "Well?"

Because shaking my head was not a valid answer, I needed to tell him why I was acting so standoffish…and stupid!

I looked up at him, swallowed nothing, mouth had gone as dry as Egypt.

He touched my cheek. "Sweetie, is everything okay?"

Oh my gosh, even his fingers smelled nice. I know that sounds creepy-gross, but they seriously did smell good. His exotic and earthy blend of sandalwood and moss went straight up my nostrils, and that threw me for a loop like whew!

Blinking rapidly, I gathered myself and eventually willed my mouth to speak. "Well," I sighed, "It's just that I had a little accident earlier." I pointed to the what-should-have-been-obvious. The ugly Illinois shaped stain clinging to the front of my once-pretty dress. I asked him, "Would you mind giving me a moment? I really need to go into the ladies room and clean up this... Eyesore?"

I was so exasperated by that point.

His eyes went down to the stain, he asked, "What eyesore?" And then he lifted both of my hands away from me. He said, "I don't see anything wrong with your dress. You look..." he paused and smiled sweetly, "...beautiful to me." He brought his brown eyes back to mine, winked, and that made me blush.

In spite of my frustration, his sweet compliments and flirty insinuations made my face break into a blushing smile. For the first time in a long time I felt butterfly wings fluttering in the center of my stomach. I became a schoolgirl seeing her summer crush on the first day of school, and in return, all I could say was thank you.

He asked, "Ready?"

I conjured a smile, accepted that I looked as beautiful as he said I did.

I said, "Absolutely." And believe me, I was.

I had arrived much too early and had waited much too long. I'd mistaken someone else for him, spilled wine on myself, and now I was much too embarrassed. So yes, I was ready. In fact, I was too ready. Too ready to get on with this date. I mean seriously; with the kind of morning I had had, I could think of nothing better than drinking barrels of wine.

He took my hand in his, said, "Right this way." and then he moved us through the crowd, lead me in the direction of what I assumed would be our private wine tasting room.

From the first time he'd introduced himself to me, he started introducing the true essence of wine to me, so I had been dying to enjoy a private wine tasting with him.

On our stroll, he started talking to me about various wines, prepping me for the array of wines we were about to taste, explaining their details with great detail.

And I listened.

He was so informative but still my ears wouldn't

comprehend. A lot of what he was saying flew right over my head.

But my eyes on the other hand; now they thoroughly enjoyed listening to every word his beautiful lips said.

Focusing on his full lips, I noticed they wore a perfect cupid's bow. That his upper lip curved inward in the center and outward on the ends and that made me want to kiss him.

Without batting a lash I stared at his lips, watched them as they moved so poetically. I especially loved how they stretched toward his dimples and exposed his perfect white teeth every time he smiled. The way his full lips cherry-picked phrases, describing how wine rinsed across the palate, lingered in just the right places, and then finally dissipated in the perfect amount of time, was salacious.

My eyes fell in love with the way his sexy mouth formed words, how he spoke about the art of fermenting grapes, and made those grapes sound better than freshly baked bread.

He had promised to train my palate; and after holding myself back from biting and licking his beautiful lips, my palate was drooling and ready to learn some new tricks.

He escorted me past various tasting rooms. All of them had been labeled with different regions, and were busy entertaining taste buds there for the sampling our best reds and whites.

At the far end of that corridor was an unoccupied tasting room that had been closed to the public. It was one of the winery's largest barrel rooms, and had been kept under lock and key.

When we stopped at that barrel room he looked down at me, we took a moment, exchanged smiles.

I focused on his face, he was so gorgeous.

His thick dark curls falling across his eyes, framed by long dark eyelashes were disarming. He was charming and virile, packaged neatly into one very muscular frame. I will say that he had always been sexy, but there is always something more seductive about a man who wears physical strength across his chest.

He reached into his pocket and pulled out a set of three keys, stuck one of them in the keyhole and then unlocked the heavy wooden door. He held the door open for me as I eased past him.

When he closed the door behind us, all sounds booming from the corridor was shut off. As if this room was padded to be soundproof, all chatter outside went mute.

Next, and without a word, he used that same key on the inside of the door. It was so quiet in there that the sound of the tumbler was amplified a hundred times. I watched his strong hand turn the small key, listened to the dull metallic thud lock us inside the room.

Standing just inside the door, I took in the entire space.

It was large and unusually shaped. Had six walls instead of four, a hexagon, not a square. All six walls were lined with used wine barrels. Barrels that looked weathered, well traveled. Their empty bodies had been carved from spicy trees, their distinctive scent perfuming the oxygen in the room.

I eased away from him and said, "I thought we were doing wine tasting today." My eyes examined his and then swept the empty room. I turned to him.

He asked, "What makes you think that we aren't?" He chuckled.

"Well, since this room is empty…" I started to ask another question but mystery slid between us, put a hand over my mouth, told me not ruin his plans, so I remained obstinately silent.

He took my hand in his, he said, "Be patient, I have something wonderful to show you."

My eyes smiled, told him okay.

He pointed across the room. My eyes followed the direction of his finger toward the barreled wall straight across the room. He led me over to that wall and then asked me if I was really ready this time. I looked up at him, wondered what this was all about. Beautiful sins and sweet secrets were swimming in his eyes, a new sign of more suspense.

Like doing a Tango, he guided me around him, turned my back to the barreled wall.

He paused. I frowned at him.

Enough was enough. I couldn't help it; I asked him another question anyway. "So... what are we doing here?"

He smiled. Strange.

I asked a new question, this time it was laced with sarcasm. "Where are the glasses, the bottles, or are we going to taste straight from the barrels?"

Eyes on my lips, he leaned in for a kiss. His lips so soft, they stuck to mine.

He blew a long, "Shhhhh." Its cool breeze drifted into my nose. I closed my eyes, quietly inhaled his fresh breath. He smiled and kissed me again. That kiss little longer, included a French gift. His warm tongue glided across mine, gave me the pleasure of tasting his fresh breath. I closed my eyes, pictured him chewing fresh mint leaves from an organic herbal garden.

There was a whispers space between us, and I felt his heat. Holding me in his arms, I felt his strength. He pulled my chest into his and took a step backwards away from the wall.

His fingers crept between two barrels and pushed some sort of button or trigger.

Quietly, like a well oiled machine, the wall of barrels slid to the left and I jerked with a hard flinch, nearly jumped out of my skin.

This date was too much, the most stressful that I had ever had.

Behind the barrels there was a gaping hole in the wall, revealing a hidden passageway.

It was a disguise.

The wall had been stacked with faux barrels concealing a secret   door.

When the barrels gave way, I moved in closer to him, sealed the last few inches that separated us.

Arms bear hugging him, my body was pressed firmly into his chest, I tucked my head under his chin.

Heartbeat and breathing in a race, I asked him, "What is this?" Looking up at him, my eyes searched for new clues, "Where are you taking me?"

I turned, looked into that gaping mystery.

His response, silence.

I let a moment pass and then repeated my question.

His lips finally animated, eyes finally came to mine, both moved in a haunting slow motion. He said, "To the place you've been dying to go."

The way those words crawled out of his straight-face, scared me.

I did my best to look unconcerned. "Oh really. Well it must be Heaven." My words came with a slight laugh.

His reaction, a careful smile followed by more haunting words. "It is."

I cleared my throat. "O…K."

And in this heaven there are no gods… and no devils… but…" He slid a strong hand around my small waist, pulled me close to him, "…there will be one angel." His hand flat against the small of my back he pulled me in even tighter, "You will be that angel." I felt the bulge behind his zipper thumping against my crotch. He put his lips close to mine, whispered, "My angel."

"But?" I turned to the hole in the wall, "What is this?"

He said, "Let's go."

"Go where?"

He kissed my lips, twice.

I shook my head, swallowed, and stared into his secrecy.

I eased from his arms, went to the doorway, touched the slope of its open threshold and peered inside.

About five feet in front of me was a spiraling stairwell traveling into the ground.

Looking into that throat of darkness, I asked, "Are we going down there?" I turned back to him, looked at his face and then past his shoulders to the door leading to the hallway, contemplated ending our date.

I said, "I don't know about this."

He touched my chin, brought my eyes back to his. He said, "Trust me."

Trust me! Is he serious? Trust me...The last two words uttered to so many victims of stupidity.

This date was not going in the direction of anything that I had imagined. When I thought of a private wine tasting all of this was the furthest thing from my mind. And even though I loved the elements of suspense and intrigue, the mystery of all felt a lot like an eerie mix of weird and wonderful all rolled up into one.

I knew he was intense and eccentric. I also knew I was strangely attracted to that part of him, so as apprehensive as I was, keeping that in mind, I decided to stop complaining and just go along with the flow.

I covered his large hand with my small palm, took a deep breath and did my damnedest to stop feeling ill-at-ease, to leave my cautious self behind. I had come this far and at this point decided to stay intrigued and curious about finding out what he had waiting for me at the bottom of those stairs.

"Okay, let's go." I looked at him with a suspicious eye and walked through the dark opening.

On the other side of the doorway was another button.

He pushed it.

The barrels slid back into place, and all went pitch black.

He moved around to the front of me, the familiar leading the blind. My breast to his back, arms clasped around his waist, eyes wide open as I tried adjusting my vision to the darkness. He inched me toward the spiraling stairwell and then I made the sign of the cross in my mind.

It was a narrow descent that had been dimly lit with tiny tea lights. Petite flames dancing along the edges of roughly carved stone steps, their little burning wicks leading the way.

It was so dark and quiet, my heels clicking against the stone steps were the only sounds heard.

We traveled about two floors below ground, ended in a

spacious grotto that had been filled with the buried treasure he wanted to share with me. We were in a cavern that felt historical. An underground hideaway that had been excavated and lined with more old wine barrels, all of them real this time, standing under candlelight. It was impressive.

He had taken me to his private sanctuary and I immediately understood why it was so special. This space felt warm and worn, old and well preserved, extraordinary and romantic.

I released my grip on him, eased around his tall body. I walked to the center of the room where three barrels stood upright, side by side like soldiers.

The first barrel held five wine glasses filled with dark violet and maroon colored wines. The barrel in the center held a silver platter of fresh fruit; strawberries, blackberries, black cherries, and grapes. The last barrel, the one on the right, held five wine glasses filled with golden-white wines.

I turned back to him, he was staring at me. For a few seconds, I stared back.

I asked, "What is this place?"

"It's an old cooling room." His voice was low, secretive.

It felt a little warm in this ex-cooling room. Not hot or suffocating, but definitely warmer than cool.

It was spacious but not imposing. Large enough to be a living room and cozy enough to be a bedroom. It was beautiful and serene.

The brown barrels glowing in the hues of warmed pecans and honey maple trees. The scent of being inside of a log cabin gave a natural sweetness that took me back to my childhood days of camping in the woods.

I folded my arms across my breast. "An old cooling room huh?"

"Yes."

I raised a brow, waited for a better explanation.

Leaning against the wall closest to the stairwell, he slid his hands into his front pants pockets, began to further explain. "This room has been here and forgotten about for years." His eyes moved around the room, my eyes followed his, "Was used by the founders of the winery as a wine cellar that held all of their prized wine making secrets. Was recorded in the original floor plans of the winery, but erased from the new blueprints during the remodel." His eyes met mine, "It's a wine cellar forgotten by many, but always remembered and cherished by me."

He spoke about this cellar, this cave, like it was his spouse. He romanticized its existence like it was his private lover, one that he had always been attentive.

Soft candlelight painted a dreamy glow all over this secret room. There were creamy candles placed here and there on the floor. The beauty of the candlelight was enhancing our moment of stillness and solitude. Our shadows casted against the barrels and rugged ceiling reminded me of something so true; there is a reason candles are integral to religious and spiritual ceremonies all over the world. Their flickering flames were mesmerizing against the barrels and the wine glasses, made the fruit look like it was picked from a picture hanging on a wall, made him look illusory, like the man of my dreams.

My eyes retraced the forgotten cooling room, took in all of its romantic beauty, snapped mental photographs of the old wine-vessels that had traveled great distances from various corners of the world: France, Italy, Spain, South Africa, and Argentina. Others stamped Portugal, Australia, New Zealand, and the United States surrounded me, stacked ceiling high, in all their grandeur.

I shook my head slowly. "Wow. So... wow." I turned to him.

He said, "Serenity."

He was right. Thanks to serendipity, he had created the ultimate serenity.

I asked, "So... Where do we go from here?"

He smiled, the candlelight marking his pooling dimples. "Well, before we get started, there are rules."

"Rules?"

"Two of them."

I smiled, shifted my weight to one leg.

Rubbing his palms together in a circular motion, he started moving toward me, said, "This is a private tasting room, with private tasting room rules, with rules that differ from all other tasting rooms." Holding up one finger, his steps slow and easy, he continued explaining the rules, "Rule number one. There will be no spitting in this room. Everything, including the wine… is to be swallowed."

I smiled. "Everything?"

He nodded twice.

I acknowledged.

"Number two. You must let go of everything unsexy, and enjoy yourself." He smiled and right then I notice something that wasn't there before; a clef on his chin. Damn, is his face constantly changing or what?

"Three. You can do with me anything your heart desires. However…" He stopped moving in my direction. Paused. His words being gathered. "One last thing," I took a deep breath. Held it. "Nevermind."

Oh my GOD! I hate neverminds!

I finally exhaled, tripped over my tongue. "And so… what about going to… um… going to Heaven?" A little nervous excitement tugged at me, made my hand rub the back of my neck.

Holding an imaginary book in the palms of his hands, he resumed his stroll, came closer to me, his foot paces measured, echoing his slow stride against the concrete floor. "Well, let's see." He pretended to flip a page. "According to my book of life, your name has been scribed right here." He pointed to the imaginary page.

At that point were now standing toe to toe. Looking down into my eyes, his baritone spoke softly. "You have been granted wings, and tonight you will fly."

Oh my Gosh.

His energy was commanding. His gorgeous face, enslaving

58

me.

I blinked, broke our stare, glanced over to the glasses of reds and fought fears of my wild imagination that there may be something crazy like GHB lacing the glasses. I shook that thought out of my head.

I pointed to the first barrel. "Syrah?"

"Syrah?"

"Yes, will we taste a Syrah?" I smiled with high hopes.

He said, "Both Syrah and Petite Sirah."

"Great. They're two of my favorites. Deep-colored, characteristics of pepper, smoke and chocolate. Right?" I flashed him a different smile, one that told him that I had paid some attention to his lessons and that I was a quick study.

"Good girl!" He congratulated me with a kiss to my lips. "I'm impressed."

Although I'd always loved the thought of wine, it wasn't until after he turned my mind that I developed a real appreciation for it. And being a born saleswoman, I had sold everything from diamonds to dreams, so before I met him, wine was just another fine item for sale.

He gestured toward the barrel holding the glasses of whites. "We will also explore Arneis, Fiano, and Chardonnay."

I perked up even more. "Sweeties from Italy and California?"

His smile broadened. "Right again!"

I tapped my lips with my finger, told him I deserved another kiss. He placed another on my lips and I melted a little bit more. I was really beginning to enjoy our little impromptu get-it-right-and-win-a-kiss game.

My new excitement was apparent, screamed let's do this. By then I had completely forgotten all about the way my day had started, could care less about my ruined dress.

He reached to his left, picked up a glass of a red and raised it as if to say cheers. "Shall we?"

"Which one is this?" I pulled the glass to my face, hovered my nose over the rim.

He said, "Barbera."

"Mmmm, Cherries and vanilla."

The bouquet was delicious, creamy. Its smell so alive, one whiff and I could almost taste it.

He put the glass to my lips, tipped it until it was empty.

I crossed my fingers 'Please don't have GHB' and then I swallowed a mouthful. I really needed to just cool it and stop with all the crazy paranoia and follow rule number two. To let go and enjoy myself. And so I did.

I let that dose of sugar and spice invade me, warm my throat for what was to come.

Holding the next glass in his hand, he asked, "Did you like that?"

I licked my lips, nodded yes.

Another red introduction. "This one is Cabernet Franc. The one that shadows King Cabernet Sauvignon."

Again he tipped his hand, draining the glass until it was empty. As he poured, some of the red liquid spilling from the corners of my mouth, down my chin, and then crawling between my breasts where his quick tongue caught its escape.

I placed my hand over my heart. Oh shit, I hadn't expected that.

His tongue was like a warm washcloth, moving in soft circles under my neck. Damn, that feels nice.

Each lick was crippling and addictive, I almost begged him not to stop.

I had been desperately craving the company of a man, loneliness and my vibrator had been my constant companion, and now I was experiencing more than my sexual fantasies had ever imagined.

I could feel the bold red staining my esophagus, infusing with my blood. That one was strong and dry, warm in my chest. Its full body rushed down my throat and then detoured up to my head. Loosened the sexual-kinks that had me knotted up.

Our tour continued and he poured and poured.

One for me. One for him.

He showered my palate with so many reds, and dropped new

kisses up and down my neck with each glass. By the time I swallowed the Petite Sirah, I was so warm with wine and kisses the warm cooling room was starting to get hot. My head started spinning, made me lose my balance. I stumbled, spun into his strong arms.

My head fell back.

Breathing relaxed. My eyes went to his.

He said, "Take off your shoes." And his wish was my command.

I kicked off my heels, pushed them to the side. That made him grow even taller.

Staring down at me, he gave a new commandment, "Open your mouth."

In that moment, his smiling face slid into a different frame, morphed into a new look. Went from charming to erotic, from Michael the cute Wine Stacker to... I don't know...Miguel.

He poured more take-control down my throat. And I gave up more-control with each swallow.

Suddenly my legs felt tingly.

There was a new passion blooming between my thighs, humidity rising to a boiling point. I wanted him to touch me there, to massage that throbbing away.

The room was rotating, wine barrels moving all by themselves. So much wine streaming through my veins, my mind started doing summersaults. I looked into his beautiful brown eyes, watched as they floated south toward my breasts. He brushed a fingertip down my left breast, feathered my nipple, and I shivered.

He kissed the back of my hand, up my arm and across my shoulder, he said, "Your skin is beautiful."

I trembled and my skin itched with heat.

Breathing lithe and easy, legs tingling, I felt wobbly and weak. My words became new, accented with a slur. I asked him, "What country are we visiting next?" words running together, painted with red and white fermented grapes.

He placed his soft lips to my ear, whispered. "The

erogenous zones." And with that, he had stamped my passport, had me ready to fly.

His finger traced up my thigh. I bit my bottom lip, anticipated.

His finger found its way under my dress, made its way to the top, and then there came a pause. His finger had discovered the unexpected; No panties under my dress.

A closet freak.

He had stumbled upon that hidden part of me.

His hand backed away and then his eyes focused in the direction of his new discovery; something soft and wet high between my thighs.

He gripped the hem of my dress, and then like a magician, he snatched it away like doing the tablecloth trick.

As quick as a flash, my strapless dress was ripped away and thrown to the floor. My full breast bounced and then settled, stared right at him.

Being pantiless had uncovered a major detail in my own secret plans.

He cupped his hands under my ass and then he kissed me. His eyes intent and hands steady, he clintched his strong jaw and lifted my body into the air. He sat my hot sex on the silver platter of cool fruit, and that jolted me. The sensation of hot and cold sent waves of electricity crawling across my flesh.

That single act of climate mixing threw me, turned the key and unlocked cryptic cravings, made my legs betray privacy, and then a moment later; my beautiful centerpiece was revealed.

Eyes starved, hands to the back of my things, he squeezed his fingers into my soft flesh, pushed my legs back, made them spread wide. Desires leading the way, he lowered his handsome face far between my knees and then licked me with one long, hot, slow stroke.

The introduction of his tongue rocked me, rearranged my thoughts. His tongue was artistic, performed pirouettes around my clit, flicked and licked up and down. I squirmed and moaned softly. He was doing the same. I shuddered from the stimulation of his breath warming my sex, of his tongue tracing the edges of my swollen lips.

I ran my fingers through his hair and drug my fingernails across his scalp as he kissed and licked and tortured me. His tongue traveled from top to bottom, from the front door of my paradise to the back door of my x-rated G-spot. He had me bending my legs, rolling my hips as my raw sugar was being harvested by his skilled tongue, being savored in indescribable ways.

The Wine Stacker came up licking his glossy lips and I thanked him with an angelic smile.

He reached between my legs, picked a piece of red fruit from the platter and then put it in his mouth.

He came to my lips, a fat strawberry carried between his, and then he shared it with me.

He fed me.

Kissed me.

Told me lies.

He made open-ended promises that most men never intend to keep. Each of his kisses insinuating that he would love me forever, that tonight was merely the beginning of something never ending.

He stepped away from me, watched me chew the forbidden fruit. I shifted on the platter, watched him remove his shirt, and then I swallowed. One button at a time his Belvedere torso was exposed, and the Michelangelo sculpture came to life; a masterpiece inspired by Hercules, the Greek god of mythology.

I marveled at him and was glad I had come. I had long forgotten about what he was going to do to me, of being so far underground. With those fears erased, I decided that here was where I wanted to be, that I wanted to stay, that I wanted to wait for his empty promises.

Four more glasses of wine, all four of them white.

With each gulp I swallowed inhibitions and lost myself more and more, started forgetting who I was.

The wine ran through me in erratic waves.

There was a tingling that started in my feet, traveled up my legs, and into my warm spot. Stomach churning, my chest heaved with an intensity that weighed me down to my knees.

His voice came to my ear, whispered, "It's happening."

His words stirred and shocked me.

I was floating into another world, felt as if I would burst, and then... I was under. A swirling tunnel of blinding color and light pulling me down like and undertow. I fell forever. Images raced by of lovers past. I fell past me as an awkward teen, dateless at my prom, and then me as the blossoming college graduate who eventually became the outwardly sexy but undersexed sales girl.

I thought to myself, What's happening to you?

Seconds later, like a cooling cascade, my alter ego was unveiled.

A personality fitting for the occasion.

The feeling was strange, and emancipation. I didn't resist, to the contrary, I embraced who I had instantly become.

My alter ego peeled her way out of me, felt like an old friend, one that I had always known existed but had long lost communication with.

She had slid her way out of me and then in a haunting whisper she announced her name.

Iradia.

Her name echoed from the center of that hallow underground womb, a voice traveling in a slithering swoosh, encircling me, encircling and him. She had come to life, had reached the surface of me, and now, she had started to breathe.

She was sexy. She was cunning. She was my gift. My gift to share with the beautiful Michelangelo; the demigod who I wanted to fuck, who I wanted to fuck me, who I wanted to fuck her, who I wanted to fuck us, who was ready to fuck who I had become.

I gave him a mythological wife, and her name was Iradia.

Leaning away from me, his eyes were caught between my legs.

His gazed was penetrating and unflinching as he unzipped his agony. He became the master of his desires, ruler of our souls.

He closed his eyes, and then I closed mine.

Iradia and the demigod, ready to consummate marriage vows.

That part of his body was well sculpted, as muscular as his arms, as wide as my fantasy, and as hard as his chest.

He broke my skin a little at a time, moved inside me at a snail's pace. Our breathing slowed, heartbeats synchronized, he eased inside me and didn't stop until he reached the top. My back was lifted into a deep arch, and he corkscrewed me relentlessly. My head was hanging upside down as our bodies danced in a perfect rhythm. Chocolate ringlets dangling behind the barrel, blood rushing my brain. Mouth open, chin to the sky, my centerpiece balanced on the silver platter of fruit. I let my eyes drift to the barrels lining the wall behind me, their words spelled backwards and upside down; I closed my eyes, listened to his paced breathing, and then I smiled at that new memory.

My eyes eased open, breath caught in my chest, I felt lightheaded, dazed, disconnected.

My world was rotating backwards, on a sphere spiraling out of control. This demigod was taking me all the way to his heaven one penetrating stroke at a time.

Ankles resting on his strong shoulders, hands gripping my waist, his head gently swayed to and fro. The calming effect of the candlelight was sacred, bringing a tranquil and restorative light to our souls. As he sank deeper inside of me, the pressure he gave was devastating, felt superhuman. He grunted with indulgence as he excavated my cave, and I churned with agonizing and pleasure filled moans

Ass crushing cool fruit, forcing their juices to waterfall to the floor, I lifted my head, found his face. My gaze went to his expression and it was marvelous. Beads of sweat blooming on his forehead like droplets of honey, and the phenomenon of flickering candle light against his bronzy skin and dark hair felt more than taboo.

Syrah, Cab, Zinfandel, and Merlot. Arneis, Fiano, and Chardonnay. Reds and whites flowing through our bodies were intoxicating. His moans mixing with mine was mysterious and eerie. Echoing. Bouncing from the stone ceiling to the cement floor. The sound of vertigo was in my ears, and I was under water, listening to what I imagined to be the sound of doves crying. He was baptizing me, making me his, making me new.

For the first time in my life I was on cloud nine and I loved every floating moment of being there.

The copper skin covering his face wore a peaceful expression, one that I can never forget.

I wanted to stroke his cheek with the back of my hand, tried to reach it, but his frame was too tall. I couldn't do it; his face was so far away.

My head fell back again, he was taking me there. Upside down tears flowing across my forehead as he went deep inside, stopped. Pulled out slow, went in fast, made small circles, pulled out slower. A torturous teasing. He did that to me over and over again.

Holding my hips tight, he made love to me, fucked me, shifted the tectonic plates of my beautiful landscape.

Our bodies in harmony, I wanted to cry.

He put my ankles together, held them up with one hand, legs closed, toes pointing toward the sky. My legs were blocking his face, obstructing my view. I couldn't see his eyes, but I had a clear view of his upper body. Watched his torso maneuver, watched his muscles work. I listened to his breathing, to his grunts and moans. I felt every inch of his climb, tongue and teeth leaving soft bites to the back of my calves. I licked my lips, squeezing my eyes tight, I tried catching my breath. He pulled out, separated my straight legs, and then bit down on my inner thigh. His head darting from right to left as his lips moved down the center of my thighs, toward the silver platter. He cupped my ass, sucked fruit juice from my sex, and my fingers road the waves in his hair as I gyrated wetness against his face.

It was slippery, it was messy, it felt incredible, but I wanted to change positions, wanted him to take me from behind.

I pushed his face from between my legs, stood from the barrel, turned around and bent over.

I put my hands behind my back, he got the message.

He put his knee between my legs, spread them wide apart. Face sideways on the silver platter, ass opened and ready to get fucked, he held my wrist like golden ropes of a chariot. He clutched my wrist together, went in hard and fast. I rocked back against his thrust and held my breath, did that to keep from screaming. Long and hard, satisfying and painful, his thrust were tranquilizing. Bodies clapping and sticking together. A mix of fruit, sex, wine, and sweat. This date needed to last forever.

Submissive.

Under his complete control, I serenaded and moaned, my song written in the key of beautiful agony.

He turned me around, slid his fingers into my hair, he told me that he wanted to see my beautiful face, to see the rising orgasms in my eyes, that he wanted to look into my panting mouth, and to imagine me sucking him while we fucked.

He lifted me back onto the platter. I released a slow, and shaky breath. Arms around his neck, heels resting on his waist, I was sitting upright but slightly reclining back.

He dipped his hips and then eased deep inside of me.

I could feel the intense pressure of his thrust, hard against the inner walls of my ass, hitting my G over and over again.

He was taking me there, dragging me with him. I could feel his spirit rising, I could see it in the painful expression written across his face. He was reaching his beautiful plateau and I could feel it as his humanity ascended into a Utopia.

Breathing rugged and uneven, his moans were primal and fierce.

Orgasmic quakes between my trembling legs, him and me, coming together, our lava stirring, erupting at once.

His forehead frowning, wearing a tender expression, my eyes half moon, I watched in disbelief as a cast of dreamy figures came and surrounded us, as they joining us in groups.

I closed my eyes, listened, thought I heard one of them singing in the distance, Hallelujah; The song written by Leonardo Cohen.

It's amazing the way dopamine triggers illusions; how it creates conscious hallucinations.

Our orgasms blending, overflowing.

A river spilling onto the silver platter of forbidden fruit, an ocean sweeter than the sweetest Sangria.

A new winemaker's blend.

A bold and decadently mysterious vintage, one so rare it would never be bottled or sold.

A mood changer crafted by a demigod.

A fine wine created by The Wine Stacker himself.

THE WINE STACKER REFLECTION...

My pallet had traveled the whole world in a day. So many regions, so many time zones. I had experienced new flavors, lands, cultures, and languages. When I finally orbited from that cave, I was serene, enlightened, completely refined.

This story is dedicated to one of my prized readers "Michael L." who is completely in love with... Wine.

A SNEAK PEEK INSIDE OF
ANGELIC'S TWISTED MIND

This story came about in a strange way. First, I want you to know that it was written in honor or Michael L., a real person, just as all of my stories are written in honor of real people. Second, I want to tell you how I came up with the concept of this story. Because of being a regular wine taster and visitor of various wineries, and after standing in the middle of so many beautiful barrel rooms (in the midst of everyday, normal people whom I've smiled and nodded at, I thought to myself, "Hmm, I wonder if..." and I let my abnormal mind do what it always does; Go bizerk! I let my imagination run wild and can't help but wonder about possible taboos happening behind the scenes of winemaking. This time it was winemaking, next time it could be God knows what. With that, it doesn't matter where I am, a winery, the beach, or even in church... I'll leave it at that. So anyway, thank you for reading, I hope you enjoyed this ride, and will stop and wonder if there is a hidden cave under the next winery that you visit.

PLATONIC

"His expression telling me I have nothing to fear; but in all reality, I have everything to fear. Finally I have realized: All that is platonic... mustn't always stay that way..." Angelic Artiaga

PLATONIC FINGERS

I've been wanting to, well, needing to share this with someone. And I can think of no one better than you.

Let me start by saying: I'm happy you're here because after months of denial, I'm finally ready to be honest. I'm no longer ashamed of the truth, of what happened, or that it was both perfect, and terrifying.

Listen.

I'm choking, but still, he whispers, "Did you like that?" I can't believe he's asking me a question like this or that he's actually done it.

I look down at my sweaty hands resting in my lap. Confused, I say, "Yes, I think so."

He whispers, "You think so?" His eyes questioning mine, his solemn brows offset by his boyish grin, making me feel a little optimistic. His expression telling me I have nothing to fear; but in all reality, I have everything to fear.

Breath caught in my throat, I find myself on the verge of choking again.

Nodding slightly, I fix my eyes on his lips and then I softly repeat my words. "Yes, I think so."

He reaches for my twiddling fingers, his hands as soft as his touch. He whispers close to my face, "I know liked it... because if I liked it... well you..." He pauses, and then - as if he's just been told something verging on hilarity - he chuckles, and I can't help thinking that he's keeping an embarrassing truth from me.

I shift and squirm on the edge of his bed, feeling extremely uneasy.

He gently cocks his head to the right, inhales, and continues from where he left off, "You must've liked it too." And then his smile dissolves into something even slyer.

My flesh crawls with tiny pimples and I feel as if I am being fondled by a million tiny fingers.

I don't want to admit it completely, so I resist and only half heartedly confess, "Yes, I think I did." And with that I manage to pull my lips into a new position; a smile that closely matches his; only difference is my smile is teetering on innocence and guilt. Innocent because I believe that I have fallen prey to him, guilt because I cannot admit my true gratefulness for having fallen prey to him.

I hate lying, and I especially hate lying to Brandon. I've always been brutally honest with him. But this time - under these circumstances - I just can't drag myself to the bold stage-of-brutality or to stand under the spotlight of truth. That will be much too embarrassing. So I play coy and keep my lips together.

I can only admit I think I liked it because I can't conjure anything more ladylike to say. Unfortunately for me, the hard cold truth is that I absolutely loved it, that it was exactly what I have been craving, that I have finally gotten what I've been quietly longing for.

That's one thing, and that's bad enough. But there is another issue, one that's an even bigger problem. A huge hitch caught deep inside the pit of my soul.

The disappointment of knowing that although I've finally gotten it, and realizing that I can't keep getting it.

Reason being.

I am not supposed to, and I'm not supposed to because it's forbidden, and we all know that things that are forbidden must to be avoided like the plague.

But I'm sorry. It was, is, so good that I was, and still am willing to suffer the consequences. I think.

I mean honestly... I can't help it.

Being with him in this way is so strong, so spiritual, so

painful, so out of control, that when it happens... I feel a sharp streak of panic, I forget how to breathe; and so, I choke.

I agree. This all must sound pretty strange, and I'm sure you're probably having a hard time understanding where I'm going with this madness. But my God... It's just that I'm so excited to finally tell somebody, to finally tell you.

My thoughts and words are running all over the place, and I really want you to understand what I'm feeling. But with so much swarming my head, I don't really know where to start.

So give me a moment. Let me slow down and gather my thoughts. I want to make real sense.

FROM THE TOP.

He, Brandon, is my best friend and closest confidant.

We are so alike. Similar personalities, ideas, daydreams, and wild fantasies amongst other things. We're both young and single, with no rings attached.

He has always been and still is, as strikingly handsome as I am beautiful. But most importantly, we had always been purely platonic friends with no romantic ties whatsoever.

IT WAS two springs ago, our favorite season of the year. A cool evening in the middle of March, the time of day when the final lingering moments of colorful daylight is prettiest, hosting a sunset so beautiful I can still see it now.

It's the evening before our small town's biggest event, the Annual Spring Festival & Art Show.

I'm just getting off work and I think of him. It's Thursday night - Applebee's thirsty-Thursday night- so I detour past his house to see what he's up to, if he wants to hang out later tonight and grab some drinks.

I pull into his drive and park my white pickup directly behind his open top, dusty green jeep. I leave my keys dangling in the ignition and head for his front porch. As I climb the three splintered steps of his porch, I notice last year's Apple Blossoms are back in full bloom. Their delicate limbs are reaching across the rickety white banister, baby pink and white petals greeting me with a soft hello as I cross toward Brandon's front door.

I touch the doorbell, but before I can fully press it, the door flies open and he lurches at me with a bang! "Hey!"

"Brandon!"I jump high and my brows drop into a deep frown, "You scared me!"

He folds his arms across his chest, chuckles at my reaction. "Did I?"

Standing tall and blocking the doorway, he's rocking with laughter. He is such the practical joker and I want to laugh, but I force myself not to. I want him to know that he has just irritated me, once again.

"Did I scare you little baby?" His rhetorical question spilling with a taunting laughter.

I'm still not laughing but then he pokes my stomach and now I'm starting to break. "Cut it out." I bat his poking finger away and roll my eyes, "You are such a boy!"

"And you are such a little girl." He bugs his eyes and wobbles his head.

Being stoic with him has never been easy, so I twist my frown into a smile.

Speaking with a playful and terrible rendition of a British accent, he straightens up and looks down his nose at me. "Would you like to come in madam?"

Shaking my head, crooked smile on my face, I look at him from top to bottom. He's wearing a white tank top, loose fitting light blue denims, bright white gym socks. He gives me a stomach another little poke with is finger, and my strained smile blooms into a cute giggle.

"I knew I would get you again." He's shaking his head, looking at me as if he's wondering why I haven't caught on to his pranks yet.

I stop giggling, frown. "I guess you heard me pull up?" My voice as dry as Nevada, the desert state Mom and I escaped when I was a toddler.

He swings the door wide and steps to the side. "Nope. Didn't hear you pull up." He is such the annoying boy and exactly as I imagine the brother I've never had would be.

"Sure you didn't." I roll my eyes and push past him.

I walk into the foyer and into a terrible mess. He's a bachelor and his living room is sure to announce that detail to every visitor upon entry. His place doesn't smell like crap but there is a lot of crap everywhere! Clothes sprawling the couches and a matching mess piled in the recliner. There are too many men's magazines and knick knacks scattered about the coffee table, and then there are the dishes crowding the kitchen countertop as they patiently await his attention for they are in dire need of a serious scrubbing.

Shaking my head behind his back, I follow him toward his bedroom. When we get to the threshold of his bedroom, I give him a little nudge in the center of his back. "Can I ask you a question?

"What?" He asks without a break in his stride.

"Have you ever thought about cleaning this place up?"

He turns his head slightly, glances at me over his shoulder and asks, "Have you ever thought about cleaning this place up?" He is all smiles.

"Are you serious?" I snap at him and nudge him again, this time a little harder.

He chuckles. "No, actually I'm not." He turns completely and looks down at me."In fact, I think sitting on that couch over there and watching you clean would be much sexier than me cleaning this mess all by myself." His eyes beam as if he has just come up with the world's brightest idea.

I start to chuckle too and then sarcasm interjects. "Now why didn't I think of that?"

"Because you're not me. A genius man." He laughs harder. "So how about it? Give me a date. Let's do this... little woman!"

Little woman!

I snap my fingers. "I know! How about February 30th?"

He turns away from me and continues his macho-man stride. I follow him into his bedroom, a cozy space that's - aside from the bathroom - the only clean room in his house. I flop down onto the side of his bed and watch him walk over to his standing ironing board.

He picks up the hot iron, pauses, and looks over at me. "February 30th huh?" he adjusts the iron's temperature.

My smirking sarcasm gives him a serious hint and then he suddenly realizes that February 30th has never been and never will be on any calendar; therefore, the day that I will clean as he sits and watches shall never come.

He sneers at me and I snip at him.

"Yes, February 30th! The perfect day for me to completely lose my mind and clean up your pig's sty!" I break into a sweet giggle and he replies with a, 'ha-ha very funny' chuckle.

I slide further onto his bed, make myself at home. His bed is blanketed with the fluffiest duvet ever. White with a pattern of rustling branches in shades of java and driftwood evoking a meditative mood that conveys warmth and flow. It's fitting to his energy. Although can be edgy and urban he is also peaceful and quiet for the most part.

He licks his finger, taps it to the hot iron a couple times and then picks up his navy and white flannel button up. He lays his shirt across the ironing board and presses the hot iron firmly into the wrinkled fabric. I watch as he drags the iron back and forth, notice the muscles on his shoulders are well defined. I stare at his shoulders as they jump and contract with every push and pull of the iron.

I ask, "Have you been working out?" my voice in the pitch of OMG!

Without lifting his head, his eyes ease over and rest onto mine. "A little bit." He turns his eyes back to his shirt and his task at hand.

Whoa! What was that look?

That's much more than a casual platonic glance, was more like a glare with an encoded message attached.

I raise my brows, almost say, 'So... how about those Lakers...' but I don't.

Instead I just throw my eyes up and trace the perimeter of

the ceiling. I sit there looking at it like I've never seen a ceiling before, marveling at its blank white canvas as if I've stumbled upon something new and interesting.

For the first time ever I feel an uncontrollable uneasiness around him. Not uneasy as in afraid, I don't have that type of fear of him. So it's not a threatening feeling; after all, he is my best friend, a very harmless best friend. The uneasy feeling that I am getting is more like an uncomfortable weirdness, one that comes with tingles in all the inappropriate places, a feeling so wrong that I don't know exactly how I should feel about it.

I break the silence, clear my throat. "Are you excited about the festival?"

His focus still trained on the ironing of his shirt, he mumbles, "Not really."

"Why not? I thought you loved the festivals."

"It's the same thing year in and year out. Dust, farm animals, hot dogs, fried pickles. Same shit, new year."

"Well, I don't know about you... but I am mad about the cotton candy." I say with an insisting smile.

He chuckles and flashes a pair of pooling dimples that are perfectly nestled into the sides of his soft shaven face. "Cotton candy," he remarks.

I nod. "Yes, the cotton candy. It's sweet and gooey... "

He stands the iron upright and snatches it's plug from the wall. "Yeah, well, I'm not going this year."

"Awww, why not?"

He shrugs his strong shoulder. "I'd rather stay home." He flashes me another telling glare.

I blink and shift. "Alone?" my question is a broken voice bordering on despair.

"Not necessarily." He winds the iron cord around the base of the iron.

What does he mean not necessarily?

He picks up his shirt, throws it around his shoulders like a cape and slips his long arms into the sleeves.

And as he is doing that, I find myself staring at the width of his chest, but then I realize that doing that is completely out of line, and so I muster the strength to look away.

I dart my eyes up to his face, he is looking straight at me – again. He's glaring at me with that same new intensity. I turn my eyes again, only this time I turn them completely away from him. I scan for a new focal point. Without delay, I find one; my eyes quickly seek refuge in the ceiling again.

He turns away from me and then my gaze instinctively returns to him. I watch him disappear into his closet and I inhale deeply.

A few moments later he reappears, work boots in hand, and his eyes are back on me.

After what feels like two eternities he smiles and then casually turns his back to me again. This is like a slow torture of wtf! He is toying with my head and I know it. I know how he operates. I know what he has done with his exes. But why is he doing this with me? He reaches for a jacket that is hanging just inside the closet and I can't take my eyes off him. My pupils leisurely travel the long distance of his tall frame. Up his strong legs, over his perfect butt, across his athletic back and then finally up to his freshly cut shiny black hair. I could feel a pool of drool flooding my mouth, I swallowed my lust and then rubbed away the tingles that were climbing the back of my neck.

Oh my gosh, what is going on here!

The looks he is giving, the body language he is using, the unspoken words, all of it has turned on a different light, hit a switch showing me the obvious. He is absolutely gorgeous. My friend has a physique that is firm and fit, amazing and strong like an action hero. I have never looked at him this way.

I turn my face, but my eyes are stuck in place. I can't stop staring at the back of his neck, the way his dark hair-line is contrasting against his smooth neck is giving me a sudden urge, the urge to stand up and touch it, to feel my his warm flesh under my fingertips as the feather down the back of his strong neck and across his strong shoulders. I am mesmerized until he looks over his shoulder at me, interrupts my twisted fantasy, his slick eyes telling me that he is reading my mind, and then embarrassment instantly rushes to my cheeks.

Caught with my hand it the cookie jar, I start chewing my bottom lip.

He issues me a sly grin and I want to run for my life.

I rub my sweaty palms up and down my thighs, try effleraging my shame away.

Brandon turns completely and faces me.

His stance is sexual. Tight abs apparent through his fitted white t-shirt, smooth chest peaking over its collar, his eyes making improper and more-than-just-friends advances at me.

He looks like a devilish Ken doll ready to play house with a new Barbie.

I shake my head, realize that I have to be out of my freaking mind. That I must be seeing things.

What am I thinking! Brandon is my plah-tah-nick friend!

He is my brother minus the biology, my secret keeper, my love-life adviser, the one who carries me through my struggles with all of my loser-guy-problems. And vice versa. I am his sister minus the mitochondrial. I had been his biggest supporter and fan since second grade, the one who advised him on his girlfriends- most of whom I happened to dislike - but that's neither here nor there.

I felt so bad about sitting on the edge of his bed, enjoying the feeling of lust growing between my legs.

But on the other hand, I felt like I was innocent. A helpless woman, caught in an unexpected and compromising position.

It had been weeks since I had been touched by a man, held in a man's arm, or felt masculine heat moving around or inside of me. So long that I chalked up my stupid illusions to be nothing more than a laughable side effect of horniness unfulfilled. And besides that, what would make me believe that he could ever be the man to cure my self-diagnosed illness.

I needed to refocus, to put my vulgar thoughts in check, to make my exit before making an even bigger fool of myself. But before I could make up a logical excuse to leave, work boots in hand, he came and sat beside me on the bed.

The weight of his body shifted the bed and so did my breathing.

I looked at my empty wrist, pat him on his shoulder. "Well, I had better get going." I said that but didn't move. The feel of his shoulder under my palm was paralyzing, so I let my hand rest there for a few moments.

He dropped his boots on the carpet in front of him, and then without a word, he leaned over and did it.

Oh! Shit!

I couldn't believe it!

He caught me off guard, and did it. Even though I wanted him to, I didn't think he would really make a move. I mean, in my perverted imagination I hoped he would, but not in real life. And the worst part is that I saw it coming, and didn't budge.

I hope this is not a test of my friendship.

His last girlfriend told him that I didn't like her because I wanted him for myself.

She was wrong.

And now he has put his lips to mine. If this is a test, I'll just play it off, tell him that I didn't see it coming, that I only saw his face moving toward mine in my peripheral that he wasn't in full focus.

But after the flirting that he had just done I did see it in a foggy denial sort of view. His glances were penetrating, oozing, left something looming like an aura, and I sensed it. Not only did I sense it, I acknowledged it and then shamefully wanted it.

Oh God. I know I must sound off. But it was just so mind blowing. And the way he did it, how it felt.

In that moment I couldn't remember how to breathe, and so that's when I choked and he asked me if I liked it.

All reality fell away, and so I didn't answer right away. That's when he leaned over, brought his face to mine, and then gradually, slowly, pressed his soft lips against mine. He eased his warm tongue past my lips and I yielded, relaxed my lips and introduced my tongue to his.

We shared soft tongue taps and gentle gliding. Smooth and sweet, with an easy friction, our tongues moved in a synchronized rhythm.

His hands in my hair, my hands eventually caressed his face as my tongue continued bending and moving under his.

I had never held his face in the palms of my hands like that before.

His kisses were clean like spring water, warm like summer, and tight like new sex.

He moves in closer to me, and I freeze... TO BE CONTINUED

To find out what happens with these two, grab the steamy novel Platonic Fingers! It's an adventure you will instantly fall in love with.

PLATONIC TEASER

His touch was soothing, almost heroic. Rescuing me from my struggles with need to orgasm. So much wetness, my honey gathered on his fingertip, and then a kiss later, that platonic finger found its way inside me. My breathing became difficult, heart rate erratic, soft kisses and masturbated sex. My hips moved with the rhythm of his hand, I was so wet. I reached for his belt buckle and then his breathing became labored.

The world was revolving around us, moving at its own pace, and at the same time dictating the pace of our exposé. We moved with the pull of the planet, gravity so strong, a pull that would require the energy of three hundred Earths to be controlled. There was no stopping the magnet between us, the attraction that was encapsulating, went from zero to ten, moving in warp drive.

He eased my shorts down my thighs and over my bare feet, and then he dropped them next to me. He lifted my black cami over my breast and then gently pulled it over my head.

I was nude. He was still fully clothed.

I felt vulnerable. So exposed. But I trusted him. He was my best friend and new lover who had not yet hurt me.

He said, "You're beautiful." And then ran his wet index finger through the space between my breasts.

I whispered, "Thank you."

He said, "Let me see," and then he touched my knees.

I stopped breathing for a moment, hesitated at the thought of letting him look at the nakedness between my legs.

I exhaled, and with that permission he eased my legs apart.

He pulled his gaze away from my face, focused on my lady

flower and then he paused. He inhaled deeply and then as if searching for the perfect words to say, he sat there for a moment in silence.

Without lifting his eyes, he said, "You are truly... magnificent, the consummate princess."

I smiled, looked down at what he was complimenting, and in my mind, I agreed. That gave me a new confidence. I was beautiful, young, soft and sweet. He was as lucky as I was, and I was as deserving as he was. We were both in search of the real thing, had gone through too many crappy relationships. The time had finally come, that not only would I, but he would get to experience the best.

He asked, "May I?"

I closed my eyes and felt him leaning in, and then I felt his soft lips giving my dewy petals a warm wet kiss. I bit down on my bottom lip, rolled my head back, inhaled until my lungs burned. I reached for him, lifted his head, brought his lips to mine, stuck my tongue in his mouth, gave him a deep kiss. He sat up, climbed out of his jeans and twisted out of his T-shirt. We were both nude, Adam and Eve in the Garden of Eden. My Adam wanting to defy what was platonic, wanting to drink nectar from my tree of life, so I opened my legs and let him. He eased my legs back, further apart, and a moment later his warm tongue started doing thing to me that I couldn't conceive, poetry and song in a foreign language, spoken from his lips to mine. I reached down and ran my hands around his head, held him there and urged him to give my flower deeper kisses. The air outside shifted, bringing a damp chill with it, that cool air slipping through the slats in the walls of the shed. Eyes sprung wide, locked on the dark space above us, I whispered into the air, pleading, alternating words, his name and God's.

Our being together felt so sinful, so delicious, so *Sinfulicious*.

I prayed mom didn't miss me, couldn't hear my sexual pleas, wouldn't come out searching the darkness for me.

Right then, in that dark and damp shed, my prayers were being answered. The sky opened wide and a fierce spring rain suddenly poured down, drowning out every sound.

Rainwater seeped through the roof of the shed, fell across his bare back, into my face. Our emotional bond was growing, becoming intertwined, a rope of physical connections and forbidden feelings, feelings that should not be shared between best friends, between the unwedded.

His head moved in a dizzying round and round motion, twisting me in to so many tangled knots. Lips crawling my stomach, tongue licking its way up to my breast, passion pooled between my legs as he climbed on top of me.

I touched his face, whispered his name, asked him to be gentle with me. He smiled, told me that was his plan.

I shivered and gasped for air as he eased his weight between my legs. A raging fire of hot excitement controlled my body, thrusting my hips forward in search of what his body was ready to give to me, but his body hesitated, kept some distance between us. He wanted to take his time, to reassure me, to tame my anxiety. All of my desires that had been pushed to the back burner and left there to simmer were now at a rolling boil. I looked at his beautiful face, his expression so gentle and sincere. I lifted my head, kissed his soft lips, and then relaxed my head back onto the floor of hay. He smiled an easy smile and his eyes told me to let everything go.

Conscious of his well endowment he was careful, sinking into me at a snail's pace, breaking my flesh little by little, I sank my teeth into his muscular chest.

My body wept slippery sweetness as it started making love to my ex-best friend, to my new lover. He was granting all wishes that I had privately shared with him, of my secret dreams of being with a man who would make love to me like I was the most perfect, most beautiful, most wanted woman in the northern hemisphere.

He asked me if I liked what he was giving me. Told me he loved what I was giving him. His thrusts were kind, his hands were gentle, his flesh poured the smell of arousal. So many sweet notes of affection were given to me, expressed to me, the way he was making love to me was beyond me. I held onto his strong body, wildly kissed his beautiful face, and in return he satisfied me like fed hunger.

My blood was quickening, thumping against my veins and my legs began to uncontrollably shake. He told me he loved me over and over again, I told him that I loved him too.

My long hair was wet with perspiration, tangled with hay.

He looked down at me, eyes wild he said those faithful words. "I can feel you coming. It's so warm..." his words trailed away.

He whispered, "I can feel you... pouring against me." He caught his breath, panted. "Can I... pour into you?"

His body stiffened, every muscle in his chest and arms contracting. I wrapped my legs around his waist pushed against his weight. He said my name and then his movements slowed, filled me with a new heat, liquid gold spilling down crack of my ass, onto the hay, and into my permanent psyche.

I rubbed his back, comforted him with a soft finish. Resting on his elbows he kissed me, asked me if I was ok. I told him that it was raining outside, but inside, lying there underneath him, I felt warm and wonderful like it was a sunny day...

"This is only the beginning of a new masterpiece that will live on its own, between its own covers. A novel called Platonic Fingers, coming soon."

PLATONIC FINGERS REFLECTION...

Being a woman who honestly enjoys true erotic romance and beautiful sex, I decided to craft this story in this way. Often times people are so thrilled about a new love, and especially a love kept hidden in the corners of their minds that when it actually comes to life we brim with excitement and can't wait to tell someone. This is why I chose the voice of a nervous girl wanting to share her experience. She was a bundle of nerves, ready to talk and express herself. I am sure you can relate. I hope you enjoyed this *sweet and soft* erotic tale. Until next time... Ciao

*This story is dedicated to one of my prized readers "Ranita V."
Who is completely in love with... Her ex-best friend.*

To have a story crafted especially for you please
visit me on the web and make your special request at;
Facebook.com/WriterAngelicArtiaga
Twitter.com/AngieArtiaga

SINFULLICIOUS YOU...

This next story is a story that I wrote with *you* in mind.

I know that everyone has a little *Sinfullicious* creativity living inside of them, and now it's time for that *Sinfullicious* you to come crawling out.

I'm going to help you to reach inside and bring it out. There is no need to be afraid because it won't hurt one bit. I think your coming out will feel so good, that you will find yourself wanting to do it again and again.

Just in case you're shy, I am going to make the first move. After I make my move you are to follow. At the end of the story you will notice that there is a ... That is your cue to take over and race to the sexy finish line. Have fun and until the next *Sinfullicious* volume...Ciao

A BIG CUP OF SUGAR

I'd made it home about an hour before he did, so I decided to relax with a bath.

I dropped my purse and keys on the couch and stopped by the kitchen where I grabbed my bathing supplies, and his sexy surprise.

A cup of dry milk, a jar of honey, a glass, and a bottle of my favorite white wine.

He had been relaxing in my mind all day long. Lounging and taking up space, moving in and out of one seductive room after another.

Today was definitely going to be the day.

I went upstairs and placed my jar of honey on my vanity. I drew my bath, and poured the cup of milk flakes into the warm water.

Glass and bottle in hand, I lifted my long hair and indulged the tub.

The warm milky suds were slick against my skin, made every part of me feel so soft. I made myself comfortable and relaxed my head onto my bath pillow.

It was quiet. Peaceful. The only sounds of life were the slow swoops of my own breathing.

I sipped my wine, meditated, and then hummed a few seductive lullabies.

Two glasses later, I heard a chirp setting a car alarm.

So I stepped out of the tub, and ran on tiptoe over to the bathroom window that overlooked the street in front of my house.

It was him, he had made it home.

I smiled at him through the window but he didn't notice me looking.

I turned and crossed my master bath, wet footsteps behind me.

I went over to my vanity, sat in front of the mirror, and took a moment to enjoy the view.

My wet, round breast, were ready to be held in the comfort of his mouth.

My shiny legs, were ready to be laced around his waist.

I dipped my finger into the jar of honey and then opened my legs... wide.

I closed my eyes, inhaled deeply, and left a sweet golden pearl drop, a delicious crowning to the rooftop of my temple of love.

I stood from my vanity, wrapped my soft damp skin with my red silk robe, grabbed the big empty cup, and headed for *his* front door.

I rang his doorbell, and waited. When he finally opened his door, I wiggled a little, and asked, "May I borrow... a big cup of sugar please?"

He stood there, shocked.

His eyes looking down at *everything* that I wanted him to see.

His admiration, unmistakable.

He smiled, "Of course."

He swung his door open and motioned for me to come in. I crossed his threshold, looked up at his gorgeous face, and then he... (The story is all yours. Now work your magic).

ABOUT THE AUTHOR

A master wordsmith of vignettes, Angelic has lots of fun teasing her readers imaginations. Creating mysterious beginnings and orgasmic endings, her arousing imagery and vivid word-play always keeps her readers drooling for more.

Please visit me on the web at:
www.AngelicArtiaga.com
Facebook.com/WriterAngelicArtiaga
Twitter.com/AngelicArtiaga
Instagram: AngieArtiaga

www.ingramcontent.com/pod-product-compliance
Lightning Source LLC
Chambersburg PA
CBHW070224140626
46555CB00018B/1267